"This is not the office," James growled at her, his expression thunderous.

"You're still my boss," Lucy countered.

"Time you stopped putting your life into neat little pockets," James told her. "Forget playing safe. Take a risk."

He caught her totally off guard, hauling her in to him with a thump that left her breathless. Or maybe it was the impact of feeling a vital wall of muscle connected to her wobbly frame that stole her ability to breathe.

"Now melt," he commanded gruffly.

And Lucy melted.

D0710206

Some of our bestselling authors are Australian!

Emma Darcy...
Helen Bianchin...
Miranda Lee...
Lindsay Armstrong...

Look out for their novels about the
Wonder of Down Under—
where spirited women win the hearts of
Australia's most eligible men.

THE AUSTRALIANS

Coming soon:

Marriage at a Price
by Miranda Lee
On sale June 2001

Emma Darcy

THE MARRIAGE RISK

THE AUSTRALIANS

HARLEQUIN®

TORONTO • NEW YORK • LONDON
AMSTERDAM • PARIS • SYDNEY • HAMBURG
STOCKHOLM • ATHENS • TOKYO • MILAN • MADRID
PRAGUE • WARSAW • BUDAPEST • AUCKLAND

ISBN 0-373-12157-1

THE MARRIAGE RISK

First North American Publication 2001.

Copyright © 2000 by Emma Darcy.

This edition published by arrangement with Harlequin Books S.A.

® and TM are trademarks of the publisher. Trademarks indicated with ® are registered in the United States Patent and Trademark Office, the Canadian Trade Marks Office and in other countries.

Visit us at www.eHarlequin.com

Printed in U.S.A.

CHAPTER ONE

'AND how is my ever delightful and worthy Miss Worthington this morning?'

Lucy gritted her teeth against a seething wave of resentment, almost hating the man who clearly had no idea how such blithely tossed off words lacerated her heart.

The breezy greeting from her boss probably meant he'd spent a highly pleasurable night with his latest woman. His voice lilted with macho smugness, a sure sign of sexual satisfaction, and his playful play on her surname accentuated the fact that Lucy wasn't the type he'd toss in his bed, however delightful she might be to work with. *Worthy* women didn't excite him.

Though if her breasts were big enough to fill and overflow a D-cup bra, he might consider her more *bed*-worthy, Lucy thought caustically, ungritting her teeth and turning from the filing cabinet to direct a bland smile at the sexy wolf who employed her as his sensible secretary.

'Good morning, sir,' she piped sweetly.

James Hancock was the classic tall dark and handsome prototype, with the potent addition of a shrewd business brain and the kind of charm that won friends and influenced all the *right* people. He was thirty-four, in the prime of life, had the well-earned reputation of being a dynamic agent in the entertainment field, which helped make him an A-list bachelor in Sydney society, and he was definitely exuding an air of being on top of his world.

His rakish black eyebrows lifted. 'Sir?'

She cocked her head on one side, returning his quizzical look. 'Weren't you cueing me to greet you formally with *your* Miss Worthington?'

He laughed, his blue eyes twinkling devilish delight. 'The comeback queen strikes again. What would I do without you to entertain me, Lucy?'

Resentment crawled down her spine and loosened her tongue. 'I imagine you'd quickly find someone else to score off.'

'Score off?' he repeated incredulously. 'My dear Lucy, the scoring honours invariably go to you.'

'Really? I hadn't noticed.'

She picked up the files she'd extracted from the cabinet and carried them to her desk, ready to hand them over to him.

'It comes naturally to you,' he assured her, grinning from ear to ear. 'One of the joys of office hours, hearing your salty down-to-earth comments. They invariably reduce all the hype in this business to what's real and what isn't. An invaluable talent.'

'Invaluable enough to be *worth* a raise in salary?'

'Ouch!' He mockingly slapped a hand against his forehead. 'She strikes again.'

'Pure logic, James,' she pointed out with limpid innocence while savagely wanting him to pay for seeing her as nothing but a bottom line sounding board when it came to dealing with his high-flying clients. 'You'll need to check these files while answering this morning's e-mails. Is there anything else you need from me right now?' she asked, pressing for him to enter his own office and leave her alone to get over the frustrations he aroused in her.

He ignored the files, shaking an admonishing finger at her. 'You're a money-grubber, Lucy Worthington.'

She shrugged. 'A woman has to look out for herself these days. I just don't believe in free meal-tickets.' Which was a neat little jibe at the women he favoured, women who traded on lush physical assets to get where they wanted.

'Ha!' James crowed. 'I gave you free tickets to tonight's charity bash.'

'Oh?' Lucy viewed him with sceptical eyes. 'You're not expecting anything of me, like being conveniently on hand to fix up some last-minute hitch with the program?'

'Completely free,' he insisted loftily.

'How novel!' She smiled. 'I might just keep you to that, James.'

'A reward for all the good work you've done in putting the program together.'

Since the tickets were a thousand dollars each and her salary was already generous, Lucy couldn't, in all conscience, imply she wasn't well rewarded for the job she did. 'Thank you. I shall look forward to relaxing and enjoying myself tonight,' she said dismissively while still doubting the tickets were entirely free of obligation.

Why would he give them to her if he didn't want her there for some reason?

His eyes twinkled. 'It will be my pleasure to see you enjoying yourself, Lucy.'

He did have a motive. She could feel it in her bones.

'Who are you bringing?' he tossed at her as he finally picked up the files she'd supplied.

'A friend.'

One eyebrow lifted teasingly. 'A male friend?'

Did he think her so sexless she couldn't have one? Lucy struggled to maintain a calm demeanour. 'Yes. Is that a problem for you?' The challenge slid off her tongue before she could stop it.

'Not at all. Glad to hear it.'

He went off smiling, carrying the files he needed, leaving the door between their two offices open so he could call out to her when he wanted to.

Lucy sagged onto the chair behind her desk, shaken by the thought his last words had conjured up. Had he suspected she only had female friends? That she might even be a lesbian, because she didn't openly adore *him* like all the other women who came through these offices?

A wave of wretched misery churned through her stomach. She should get herself out of this job. It was eating up any kind of normal life she might have, being with James Hancock every working day, constantly wanting him, being jealous of every woman who took his eye.

He was never going to view her as anything other than an efficient secretary. Eight months she'd been with him—eight months of a helpless sexual awareness she couldn't control or even dampen. Lust at first sight, she now thought with sick irony, and it hadn't worn off.

No other man had ever drawn such a strong physical response from her. In fact, she had never really understood why other women got themselves in such a mess over men, losing all perspective and self-respect, too, when they were badly let down. *Being sensible* had been Lucy's long-held belief on how one should conduct one's life. Indeed, her mother had drilled it into her from early childhood and Lucy had come to see it saved her from a lot of grief.

But *being sensible* couldn't seem to override what James Hancock made her feel. Over the years she had admired the physiques of other men, but it wasn't just physique with James. Somehow he emanated a sexual energy that was quintessentially male, and as much as she'd tried to block it out, it always got to her, stirring up a hornet's nest of hormones.

Despairingly she propped her elbows on the desk and rested her head in her hands. The truth was, she didn't feel she really belonged to herself any more, and she didn't like the person she was becoming. What right did she have to think bitchy thoughts about women she didn't know, just because James favoured them over her? It was pure sour grapes and if she didn't stop it, she'd end up sour all through.

She should move on. Give in her notice and go.

It was the sensible thing to do.

Today was Friday. First thing Monday morning her resignation would be on his desk.

No doubt James would have his latest gorgeous model on his arm tonight at the charity ball for the Starwish Foundation, and no doubt it would ram home to her how hopeless it was to spend any more time craving what would never be available to her.

Come Monday she would definitely have screwed herself up to hand in her notice and put James Hancock behind her. For good!

So...she was bringing a man. Interesting to see what kind of man Lucy favoured, James told himself as he settled at his desk and switched on the computer. She never chatted about her private life and he couldn't deny he was curious. Most women opened up to him but not Lucy.

She was one very buttoned up lady who never lost her head over anything. Which made her the perfect assistant in his line of work, with half his clients all too ready to throw a fit of temperament if any little upset occurred. Put Lucy in the eye of a storm and she could ground everyone in no time flat by coming up with the most sensible response to the situation.

An accountant he decided. That was the kind of

man Lucy would approve of—a nice, safe accountant, solid and dependable, someone who'd never broken a law in his life and never would, a nine-to-five man, regular in his habits, serious-minded, considerate of her needs, probably wore spectacles with fine gold rims and very conservative clothes. That was Lucy's taste—neat and conservative.

James nodded to himself as he brought up the e-mail inbox on the monitor screen. He was sure he was right but Lucy had been with him eight months and all that time there'd been an elusive quality about her that nagged at him. More so, the longer they'd been together. It was worth giving her the tickets to get those tantalising flashes of something else brooding behind Lucy Worthington's buttoned up exterior sorted out in his mind.

He'd even started thinking about her when he was with other women, missing her sharp wit, wondering what she might be like in bed. And that had to be stopped. He was not going to mess with the best secretary he'd ever had. Besides which, Lucy would probably be horrified at some of the thoughts he'd been harbouring lately. Seeing her with a man of her choice—almost certainly an accountant—would definitely affirm her not-to-be-played-with status.

The telephone rang. He picked up the receiver.

'Buffy Tanner for you on line one,' Lucy stated crisply.

'Thank you.' He smiled as he pressed the button to take the the call. Nothing hidden about Buffy. She let it all hang out. And that was fine by him. Very relaxing.

'Hi, Buffy,' he said warmly, bringing her lush curves to mind.

'James darling, I'm sorry to be calling you in business hours, but I might not be able to catch you later. What time did you tell me I have to be ready by for tonight?'

He winced. Punctuality was not Buffy's strong point. 'Seven-thirty. And we must leave on the dot. I did warn you.'

She sighed. 'I have a long shooting schedule today. A new swimwear range at Bondi Beach. I'll be a mess. Will it matter if we're a bit late?'

'Yes, it will matter. It's my people doing the show tonight. I have to be on hand. If you want to cry off…'

'No, of course I don't.'

He could hear her pouting. A very sexy pout it was, too, but right now he felt impatient with it.

'Seven-thirty, Buffy. Be ready or I'll go without you,' he said irritably and cut the connection, thinking Lucy wouldn't keep her man waiting. She was a very precise time-keeper, always ensuring that appointments were kept.

With a niggling sense of discontent, James applied himself to answering the e-mails that required an immediate response. He worked through them, adding the printouts to the files, making notes of things for Lucy to check. She never slipped up on details, which was another thing he liked about her.

He could count on Lucy getting things right. No excuses. Meticulous attention to detail.

He called her into his office, his instructions already clipped onto the files for her attention. He smiled over his own judgement of her as she walked in, wearing her all-purpose navy suit, smart, classic, timeless, typical of what a sensible career woman would buy. It would take her anywhere and never go out of fashion.

The skirt ended modestly, just above her knees. No micro-minis for Lucy. Yet what could be seen of her legs—nicely shaped calves and fine ankles—suggested the full length of them could form quite a distracting sight. Just as well they weren't on show, James told himself, mentally approving her choice of apparel which neatly skimmed her cute little figure.

Being below average height, Lucy could never be called statuesque, but she was certainly built in pleasing proportion, and the way she twitched her pert bottom at times was definitely distracting. And tempting. James stifled these wayward thoughts and fixed his gaze on her face.

It was a finely boned face, not strikingly pretty, though if all the make-up tricks of a beautician were applied to it, James fancied it could look quite stunning. It, also, was perfectly proportioned, though the spectacles she wore gave it a prim look, which was accentuated by the way her hair was pulled back and pinned into a chignon from which no tendrils *ever* escaped.

The thought of unpinning what was obviously a wealth of soft brown hair presented a tantalising prospect. Would Lucy come undone in other ways? And if he took her spectacles off, what would he see in her eyes?

As it was, all he saw was a bright intelligence looking at him expectantly, nothing but business on *her* mind.

Piqued by her apparent indifference to what many other women considered his attractions, James found himself blurting out, 'Is he an accountant?' and could have instantly kicked himself for letting her get under his skin to this extent.

Her smooth creamy forehead creased as her eyebrows lifted above the colourless rims of her spectacles. 'To whom are you referring?'

Instead of dismissing the slip—the only prudent thing to do at this point—James lost his head completely to a potent mixture of compelling curiosity and a rebellious rush of seriously displaced hormones.

'Your partner for the ball tonight,' he shot at her.

She looked incredulous. 'You want to know if he's an accountant?'

'Is he?'

'Do you need an accountant on hand for some reason?'

'No, I don't *need* one.'

Her eyes narrowed in suspicion. 'Then why are you asking?'

Why, indeed? James gritted his teeth. He was getting no satisfaction here and was fast making himself look foolish. His mind zapped through possible escape routes.

'Conversation always goes more smoothly if I'm prepared with a knowledge of people's backgrounds. Your partner is the only one I won't know at our table.'

She stared at him. Her chin took on a mulish tilt. Her shoulders visibly squared. In fact, her whole body took on a tense rigidity. Even her hands clenched. James had the wild notion she was barely stopping herself from stepping forward and hitting him. Which, of course was ridiculous! He'd made a reasonable statement. He *did* like to be prepared with background information before meeting anyone. She knew that.

Though he had to concede this was more personal than professional ground. Her private partner wasn't exactly his business. Maybe it was simply the effect of the glass lenses but her eyes looked very glittery and he was definitely sensing some dagger-like thoughts being directed very sharply at him. But dammit all! He was going to meet the guy tonight so what was she getting so uptight about?

'Why do you think my escort for the ball is an accountant, James?' she bit out, her voice dripping with icicles.

'Well, is he?' he persisted, frustrated by her evasive tactics.

'Generally speaking, people consider accountants

boring,' she stated, once again denying him an answer.

'Not at all. Obviously they're very intelligent, very clever, very astute,' he put in quickly.

'Boring,' she repeated as though she was drilling a hole in his head. 'Boringly worthy for Lucy Worthington.'

Uh-oh! James saw the red rag waving. He instantly gestured appeasement. 'Now, Lucy, I have never thought you boring. You know that,' he pressed earnestly. 'And I can't imagine you tolerating a boring man. You're taking this the wrong way. I was merely wondering...'

'What kind of man I'd bring.'

The intense focus of her eyes was like an electric drill, sparks flying as it kept tunneling into his brain to the true core of his question. James shifted uncomfortably. He didn't like the sense of her seeing right through him. No doubt about it—he'd dug himself a hole and somehow he had to climb out of it with some fast face-saving.

'It would be helpful if you'd give me his name, Lucy,' he said reasonably, dropping the background issue which had stirred her into this totally unacceptable attack. 'It would save any slip-up with introductions.'

Her mouth thinned. Her eyes glittered even more sharply. He sensed her fierce urge to cut him to ribbons and perversely enough—given the tricky situation he'd brought upon himself—he felt quite pumped up by the passion she was emitting. Nothing

cool and collected about *this* Lucy. Clearly he'd
tapped into the real flesh and blood woman beneath
the navy suit and James found himself actually getting excited—aroused by the prospect of the inner
Lucy emerging. If she did step forward to tangle
with him physically...

'Josh Rogan,' she said.

'What?'

'You asked for his name,' she tersely reminded
him.

James gave himself a swift mental shake as de-
flation set in. The navy suit had won again, damn
it! The Lucy he'd wanted to experience was in full
retreat. Which was just as well, he told himself,
quelling the madness of imagining her sprawled
across his desk while he satisfied a rampant desire
for the most intimate knowledge of her. It was absurd to have this sudden burst of sexual fantasies
about his secretary when he had Buffy Tanner more
than willing to satisfy his carnal needs.

'Josh Rogan,' he repeated, grateful that Lucy had
her head on straight and was heeding what was appropriate in the work-place between boss and secretary. However, something about the name she'd
given niggled him. 'Isn't there a lamb curry called
Josh Rogan?'

He was almost sure of it, the suspicion instantly
growing that Lucy was paying him back by giving
a false name that would embarrass him when he
used it tonight.

'No,' she said with a fine edge of scorn. 'The curry is called Rogan Josh.'

'Oh!' He frowned. Was she playing him up or not?

Her mouth softened and curled. 'Actually, I don't think Josh would mind your confusing him with the curry.' Her hips gave a wicked little wiggle as she added, 'He is hot stuff.'

Hot stuff? Lucy with *hot stuff*? Unaccountably James felt his temperature rising. 'I'll keep that in mind,' he snapped. 'You can take these files now. I've made notes for you.'

'Fine!'

She smiled at him as she stepped forward and scooped them up from the desk. Then she sashayed out of his office with all the feline grace of a cat, waving its tail in his face.

James sat brooding over this aspect of Lucy Worthington for some time. He was definitely right about her. There was much more to Lucy than met the eye. The navy suit was nothing but a front, de-signed to put him off seeking the real truth about the kind of woman who burned inside it.

Good thing he'd given her those free tickets. It was going to be interesting—illuminating—to see how she behaved with her *hot stuff* tonight. Hair down, sexy dress, full make-up on, no spectacles…if her Josh Rogan was truly *hot stuff*, he'd expect that of her.

A zing of anticipation tingled through James. It had nothing to do with looking forward to having

Buffy Tanner on his arm tonight. He didn't even think of the swimsuit model with the lush curves and sexy pout.

Tonight he was going to see the unbuttoned Lucy Worthington in action!

CHAPTER TWO

Lucy was still boiling mad as she stomped up the stairs to her first-floor apartment in Bellevue Hill at six o'clock that evening.

An accountant!

A boring old accountant!

O-o-o-o-h, she wanted to punch James Hancock's lights out with Josh tonight. She wanted to see him sitting at their table, looking like a stunned mullet as *her* partner outshone him, which Josh was perfectly capable of doing, the ultimate party guy when he was in brilliant form—huge charisma, pouring out his energy in bursts of winning charm. *And* he was as handsome as sin.

It was handy that he lived right next door to her in this old apartment block. All she had to do was ask and either Josh or his partner, Larry Berger, would help her with anything she needed help with. *Gay* men, she had decided long ago, could make the very best friends for a woman.

Even before she had known Josh was *gay*, back in their school days, she had really liked him as a person and they'd been good friends. He was kind and sensitive and supportive, as well as being great fun.

She had been grateful to have him as her boyfriend then, being able to go out as a couple without any of the hassle of being pressured to have sex. Some boys could get mean and nasty in pushing their wants. Some men, too, she'd found in later years. Even the few relationships she'd enjoyed for a while had lost their shine with the build-up of selfish demands. On the whole, her mother was right. Men wanted women on their own terms and *being fair* didn't come into the equation.

Josh was always sweet relief from all that. His company had no price-tag on it. He was safe and safe was good. She couldn't get into any trouble with Josh Rogan. He didn't feel any sexual desire for her and she didn't feel any for him. In fact, he was the perfect foil to her ungovernable feelings towards James Hancock, whom, in her wilder fantasies, she'd like to handcuff to her bed and watch him go mad with lust for her.

Which she knew was absurd!

James Hancock was never going to see her as anything but his *worthy* secretary. But no way was she going to let him think the only man she could attract was a boring accountant!

Having emerged from the stairwell, she bypassed her apartment door and strode straight to Josh's, ringing his doorbell with an emphatic need for a swift response.

He was satisfyingly prompt in opening the door. 'Lucy love!' His eyebrows arched over merry brown eyes. 'A change in plan?'

'Yes,' she snarled as a fresh rush of venom spilled

onto her tongue. 'My beastly employer thinks my escort this evening will be an accountant.'

'Like…boring?'

Very quick on the uptake was Josh. 'Exactly,' she confirmed. 'In retaliation I told him you were *hot stuff.*'

'Absolutely! When I'm hot I literally sizzle with high octane energy. You want me to sizzle?'

'I want you to burn him up. And Josh, wear that gorgeous metallic waistcoast and the blue silk tie.'

'A touch of flamboyance with the formal suit?'

'Shining is the order of the night.'

'Lucy love, I shall glitter for you.'

'Not too much,' she warned. 'You're not to let anyone guess you're gay.'

'Totally straight behaviour, I promise.'

She heaved a sigh to relieve all the horrid pent-up feelings James Hancock had left her with today. 'I need to get that guy, Josh.'

'In more ways than one I gather.'

She eyed him wryly. 'Hopeless case, I'm afraid.'

'Oh, little miracles can happen.' He grinned, glee-ful mischief twinkling in his eyes. 'Trust me. We'll make the man see you in a different light tonight.'

'I'll still be me, Josh.'

'And so you should be. It's his vision at fault, Lucy love, not you,' he assured her. 'Now go and put your glitter gear on and practice some sultry looks in the mirror. If I sizzle and you simmer…'

Despite the dejection that had suddenly overtaken her anger, she laughed at the picture he painted. 'I'm not exactly a sex-pot and *he'll* be with one. Buffy Tanner, the swimsuit model with the overflowing D-cup.'

Josh gestured an airy dismissal. 'You're fixated on big boobs. Superficial padding.'

'Padding or not, I wish mine were bigger.'

'*Sexy* is more in the attitude than the equipment,' came the knowing advice. 'And one other thing. Best to turn up late.'

'I'm never late. I don't like being late,' she protested.

Sheer wickedness sparkled back at her. 'But I'm hot stuff, Lucy love, and you just couldn't resist having me. Punctuality shot to hell!'

She couldn't help laughing again. 'I doubt he'd even notice, Josh.'

'Oh, he'll notice all right.' He waggled his eyebrows as he elaborated. 'His predictable little secretary suddenly not fitting the frame he's put her in. Believe me. He'll notice.'

'Well, I don't actually *need* to be there on time,' she argued to her obsession for punctuality. 'He did say the tickets were free, no work-strings attached.'

'There you are then,' Josh asserted triumphantly. 'Off you go. I'll bring you a gin cocktail at seven-thirty. Some Mother's Ruin to put you in the right party mood.'

They should be leaving at seven-thirty, her time-keeping brain dictated. It would take half an hour to get from Bellevue Hill to Darling Harbour, park Josh's car, walk to the Sydney Convention Centre where the fund-raising ball was being held in the main auditorium. Cocktails in the foyer from eight o'clock the tickets read.

But so what if she had a cocktail here? The world would not come to an end if she didn't turn up on the dot of eight o'clock. Why not be unpredictable for once?

'Okay. And thanks, Josh.' She flashed him an appreciative smile. 'A friend in need is a friend indeed.'

The very best of friends, she thought warmly as she left him and let herself into her own apartment. Even this place, which was now hers—with a hefty mortgage—Josh had advised her was a good buy, if she could scrape up the money. The previous owners, now a divorced couple, had wanted a quick sale, and Lucy had stepped into a bargain, considering the real estate values in this location, midway between the inner city and Bondi Beach.

Walking into her very own space always gave her spirits a lift. James Hancock could call her a money-grubber as much as he liked. At least she didn't have to depend on a man to provide her with the security of a home, which wasn't secure at all if there was a divorce. Her careful savings over the years had added up to a solid down payment on this apartment. She was now a woman of property and she'd achieved it by herself.

Her mother was definitely right.

Being sensible did bring its own rewards.

Yet as Lucy headed for her bedroom, she wished

she had splashed out and bought a glamorous gown for tonight. Although her one little black dress was perfectly adequate for any evening engagement, it was...*boring*. Not that it really mattered, she told herself. It was still a classy dress, bought cheaply from a secondhand designer boutique, and it would do...once again. She couldn't compete with Buffy Tanner anyway. No point in trying. And the money saved would go towards buying the furniture she wanted.

All the same, she felt vaguely disgruntled with her basic common sense as she set about getting ready for the charity ball. It would undoubtedly give her considerable satisfaction to flaunt a flamboyant Josh as her partner tonight, hopefully delivering a metaphorical slap in the face to James Hancock and his opinion of her private life. But the truth was she never did do anything wildly exciting. Perhaps she was overly careful in her weighing up of whether a step was worth taking or not.

The worthy Miss Worthington...

The words stung.

The urge to act in a totally unworthy and outrageous way suddenly held a highly tempting attraction. Especially in front of James Hancock. Free tickets meant free from any responsibility. She could play as fast and as loose as she liked with Josh, knowing there'd be no nasty consequences from him, and if she was going to hand in her notice and find another job, why not do and say anything that came into her head. Puncturing James Hancock's complacent judgement of her would go a long way towards salving her pride. And hurt.

Lawless Lucy…

She chuckled over the name that had slid into her mind.

Why not?

She stopped burning and started simmering. *Attitude,* Josh had said. Never mind her clothes or anything else. It was all in the attitude.

It wasn't like Lucy to be late.

James Hancock couldn't stop himself from glancing at his Rolex watch yet again. Another few minutes and the crowd of guests enjoying cocktails in the foyer would be moving into the auditorium. She should have been here at least half an hour ago. While he'd been waiting for her to arrive, he'd greeted an endless stream of the beautiful people and he could feel his smile getting very stiff. Damn the woman! Where was she?

His buoyant anticipation had slid through a frazzle of frustration at her continued non-appearance and was now descending into nagging worry. Had there been an accident? Lucy didn't drive, didn't own a car—too penny-pinching to buy one—but he knew nothing about this Josh Rogan who was bringing her here tonight. If he was *hot stuff* behind a wheel and had involved Lucy in a smash…no, surely she was too level-headed to go out with a speed-jerk.

But what was keeping her?

'Wow! *Who* is *that?*' Buffy breathed, her sexual interest obviously stirred.

James snapped out of his introspection, his male ego somewhat piqued. While Buffy might still be a bit miffed about his lack of appreciation for how long it took to look her fabulous best for him, drooling over other men was hardly designed to win his favour. It was as rude as unpunctuality, another black mark against continuing the relationship.

With a jaundiced eye, he looked where she was looking and was instantly jolted into electric attention. Lucy! Hanging onto the arm of a guy who could be cast as the romantic lead in a movie, and probably *was!*

He had a matinee idol face framed by a riot of black curls, a smile a dentist would be proud of, and he certainly didn't mind drawing attention to what was obviously a gym-toned body, wearing a flashy waistcoat with an over-lustrous coloured tie which mocked the regular black bow-ties most of the other male guests, including himself, had automatically used.

A young trendy show-off, James was telling himself, just as Buffy heaved a sigh that undoubtedly set her opulent breasts aquiver for the approaching sex symbol to notice. His teeth grated together as he switched his attention to Lucy, who, he was suddenly pleased to see looked her normal self—hair neatly tucked up, glasses on, the same little black cocktail dress she invariably wore when called upon to attend an evening function.

Except there was something different about her—
a jaunty self-satisfied sway to her hips—which
struck him as decidedly un-prim. Her mouth, too,
seemed to have a more sensual purse to her lips as
she gazed up at the self-styled *hot stuff,* who was
apparently amusing her with his playboy patter.

In fact, James began to feel that Lucy's prim fa-
cade was more innately provocative than Buffy's in-
your-face femininity. It was certainly tantalising,
posed next to the party guy who was parading her
towards the group in which James and Buffy stood,
waiting to be joined by these two last table com-
panions.

Waiting, James thought irritably, able to dismiss
his concern over Lucy's absence now. No doubt it
was the star act she had in tow who had kept them
waiting. He struggled to adopt an affable manner for
performing introductions, hoping Buffy would stop
ogling and have the decency to remember who her
escort was.

'Ah!' he drawled with a bright, welcoming smile.
'Here you are! We're about to go into the auditorium,' he couldn't resist adding to point out their
lateness.

'But there's time for introductions,' Buffy pressed
eagerly, positively jiggling with eagerness.

'Lucy…' James invited, keeping his teeth
clamped in a smile.

'James Hancock, Josh Rogan,' Lucy obliged with
commendable economy.

James braced himself to return a macho hand-

shake but apparently the younger man felt no need
to prove himself stronger than Lucy's employer. He
simply radiated self-assurance, his dark eyes twinkling the kind of focused interest that made people
feel at ease and pleased by the interest. James rec-
ognised the ploy. He used it himself. Josh Rogan
was clearly an accomplished salesman.

'A pleasure, having you with us,' James rolled
out, containing his curiosity while he did the honours. With a sweep of his hand encompassing the
group around him, he went on, 'I think you're all
acquainted with my punctilious secretary, Lucy
Worthington.' *Although she had certainly not been
punctilious tonight!* 'Josh, this is Buffy Tanner...'

Buffy leaned over as she took Josh Rogan's hand,
giving him an eyeful, but unlike most men who
would find the view irresistible, Josh smiled into her
face and repeated her name with a happy lilt that
could have been applied to a Matilda or a Beatrice.
If he was receiving Buffy's signals, he had no in-
tention of answering them.

The other three couples in their group were given
the same treatment by Josh Rogan as he was introduced to them. James could find no fault in his manner. The response to him was instinctively positive,
an attractive person putting out pleasant vibrations
and getting them back.

'What business are you in, Josh?' Hank Gidley,
the last one to be introduced, inquired with keen
interest.

'Fine wines. Import and export,' came the answer

that allowed James to slot him into place, though it wasn't the place he'd first imagined. However, it did explain the polished savoire-faire displayed so far. Josh Rogan was used to dealing with customers who could afford to buy fine wines and he probably charmed them into buying whatever he wanted to sell.

'Oh, I thought you'd be in modelling like me,' Buffy gushed.

The dark eyes twinkled at her wickedly. 'Like everyone else, I admire external beauty, Buffy, but I'm really into tasting superb content.' And he swung his gaze to Lucy as though she provided the taste he most relished.

She grinned at him—grinned like a Cheshire cat who'd just been fed lashings of cream—and James felt his stomach clenching with outrage. Here he'd been worrying about her, while she had been revelling in being tasted by this wine buff, no doubt with much sensual appreciation. Which explained why her hips had been swaying with that smirk of satisfaction about them.

'Time to go in to our table,' he announced tersely, and wrapped Buffy's arm around his to lead off their little procession.

Nothing was going to plan this evening.

Nothing!

And he didn't like it one bit.

CHAPTER THREE

As THEY followed James and Buffy into the auditorium, Lucy was still laughing inside at the way Josh had complimented her *content*. It was all she could do not to burst out in spluttering amusement. James had been positively tight-faced about Josh preferring her to *his* trophy woman, and Buffy Tanner's jaw had literally dropped at being so cavalierly dismissed in favour of Lucy Worthington.

A double blow to ego, she thought sweetly, and it served them both right—James for calling her his punctilious secretary on what was supposedly her night off, and Buffy Tanner for thinking she could vamp Josh right under Lucy's nose.

However, her amusement didn't last long. As they trailed after the leading couple towards their designated table, Lucy had to concede Buffy looked absolutely stunning, even the back view of her which she was swishing in front of Josh right now. The white beaded evening dress she barely wore was cut almost to her free-flowing buttocks, leaving a lovely curve of naked spine on display, and her shining mane of black ringlets dangled to just below her shoulder-blades, tempting touch.

The gleaming expanse of naked skin was without blemish, and Lucy couldn't really bring herself to believe there was any cellulite hidden under the clingy fabric that moved so enticingly with every step forward. It was all very well to feel smugly pleased that Buffy couldn't hook Josh with her seductive padding, but she did have James securely at her side.

With so much femininity on display and available to him, why would James even bother to look at his commonplace secretary in a different light? It wasn't really feasible, Lucy decided, although Josh had certainly delivered a surprise impact out there in the foyer. That, in itself, was some balm to her wounded pride.

She told herself to be content with it because miracles were not about to happen on her behalf tonight. Better to concentrate on enjoying herself with Josh than burn herself up, hankering after what was never going to be with James Hancock.

The auditorium seemed vast—a sea of tables for ten set around a dance-floor. Four hundred guests were pouring in, settling around the starched white table-cloths which added the required class to the gleaming cutlery and glasses and the centre-pieces of angel candles set in clusters of perfect camellias. Countless silver stars hung from the ceiling, a reminder that this ball was being held by the Starwish Foundation to raise funds for children with cancer.

James had organised the entertainment, free of charge, and a young, up-and-coming band was on stage, enthusiastically playing a jazzy number to get everyone in a party mood. Behind the musicians on an elevated platform was a gleaming red convertible, an Alpha Spider sports car which was to be raffled tonight, a prize to promote the idea that in every heart is a hope for something special to magically happen to them.

A wish come true was the theme of the charity ball, but Lucy couldn't, in all honesty, believe her wish that James could suddenly find her desirable had any possibility of coming true. He might wonder how a man like Josh could find her attractive, but why would that niggle of curiosity alter what he felt—or rather, didn't feel—towards his secretary?

Sex appeal was a chemistry thing and Lucy just didn't have the right elements to spark that kind of interest from him. Eight months of purely platonic treatment should have drummed that into her.

Ahead of them, James ushered Buffy to a chair at a table which had a direct view of centre-stage, one row back from the dance-floor. A prime position, Lucy thought, which, of course, James was adept at manoeuvring for himself.

'You next to me, Lucy,' he directed, nodding to his left, having already seated Buffy on his right.

Lucy was dumbstruck and instantly agitated by having to be so close to him all night. It would be sheer torture for her, almost touching, forced to hear how he spoke to Buffy, made excruciatingly aware of the contrast in his manner towards herself.

She had expected him to give his friends the more favoured places facing the stage. She was, after all, only his secretary. However, no-one protested as he organised the rest of the seating and Josh led her around to their designated chairs, murmuring in her ear, 'Guests of honour, Lucy love. Score one to us.'

Lucy couldn't accept that highly hopeful interpretation. It was too far out of step with the all too painful truth of what she *knew*. She suspected a purpose that had nothing to do with any newly noticed womanly charms. The moment James settled on the chair beside her she muttered to him, 'Why did you put me here?'

His blue eyes sliced to her with a glittering intent that cut into her heart. 'Why not?'

'You said I wasn't wanted for work tonight.'

'You aren't.'

'You've placed me on hand, right next to you.'

One eyebrow lifted in mocking challenge. 'Is that offensive to you?'

'No, of course not,' she quickly denied, although she hated—violently hated—being trapped in this position.

'Is it beyond the realms of your imagination that I might enjoy your company outside of work?'

Lucy flushed, intensely embarrassed by a directness that hit on her own secret desires. 'You've got company,' she pointed out, nodding to Buffy who was busy eyeing Josh with rapt admiration.

'I'm greedy,' James replied, totally unabashed at admitting to wanting both women to entertain him. 'It's my table, Lucy. I'm entitled to arrange it how I like.'

'What? Beauty on one side and brains on the other?' she couldn't stop herself from sniping.

His mouth curled. 'I wouldn't put it quite like that.'

'How would you put it?' she challenged fiercely, completely losing her cool as resentment of his selfish decision raged through her.

His gaze flicked to Josh, then back to her. 'Interesting to think of what caused you to be late, Lucy,' he drawled. 'Somehow I doubt it was intellectual conversation.'

Shock zapped her mind for several seconds. Then a wild welling of triumphant glee billowed over the shock. It had worked! Bringing Josh and being late *was* making James see her differently. At the very least he no longer had her pigeon-holed as his worthy secretary. She was now an interesting woman!

A smile tugged at her lips and broke into a full-blown grin. 'It's such a pleasure to feel free of responsibility, I just let my head go,' she airily explained.

'Heady stuff...wine-tasting,' he remarked sardonically.

Another jolt as Lucy realised he was actually thinking *sexual* tasting. Which was hilarious in one sense, given Josh's inclinations, yet deliciously satisfying in another, given the erotic images James was now applying to her.

She giggled. It was the wrong thing to do. She should have simmered. Josh's advice had been spot on so far. If she was to strengthen the result that had been attained, she had to project a sexy attitude. To cover the sensuality gaffe, she snatched up the glass of champagne a circling waiter had poured and lifted it in a toast.

'To tasting more of the best,' she cried recklessly.

He picked up his glass and she could have sworn his eyes simmered as he said, 'Perhaps the best is yet to come. One has to taste a range of bottles to know which gives the ultimate pleasure.'

'I'm sure that's true,' she agreed, her fantasy world swiftly building a line of gorgeous men with James placing himself at the end of it, ready and willing to show her he was the best.

'What's true?' Buffy interjected.

Lucy's fevered mind snapped back to sober reality. Seeing her differently didn't mean that James found her any more attractive. He might be intrigued by the light Josh had supposedly shed on her private life, but Buffy was his choice for *his* private life. She scrambled for a sensible answer to the question asked.

'You need to sample a lot of different wines before judging which pleases the palate most,' she eventually managed, turning to Josh for his support, wanting him to carry the conversation while she recovered some equilibrium. 'Isn't that so, Josh?'

'Absolutely,' he chimed in. 'Though I must say the very finest do stand out, once tasted.' He slid Lucy a mischievously intimate glance. 'Unforgettable.'

The urge to giggle again almost made her choke

on her champagne. Josh had obviously been eavesdropping on her conversation with James and was deliberately stirring the hot-pot, being wickedly suggestive. She controlled herself enough to sip the champagne, pretending nothing of any great note had been said.

'Do you do wine-tasting too, Lucy?' Buffy asked.

She constructed a gently dismissive smile. 'Not really. Josh occasionally shares his experience with me.'

That should have been an end to it. However, her partner in pretence decided he'd been thrown the ball and it was his job to run with it as provocatively as he could.

'Lucy uses me shamelessly, Buffy,' he declared. 'As far as she's concerned, I'm on call to deliver—' he paused to slide Lucy a salacious look '—anything she wants...when she wants it.'

Lucy kicked him under the table. He was exaggerating their relationship and making 'the wants' sound far from innocent.

'And do you?' James asked somewhat dryly.

'If it's humanly possible,' came Josh's fervent reply. 'An invitation to be with Lucy is a gold-card guarantee of pleasure.' He sighed and shook his head at her as he added, 'I wish she didn't keep herself to herself as much as she does.'

She kicked him again, forcefully warning him he was overplaying his hand, but his eyes were dancing merrily and she knew he was having too much fun to desist.

'So Lucy calls the shots in your relationship,' James commented.

'Very strong-minded lady,' Josh confided. 'When Lucy sets her mind on a path, you either fall in with her or get off.'

'Now come on, Josh,' she chided, feeling she had to scale down his assertions about her. 'I'm not that inconsiderate of you.'

His hands lifted in an eloquent gesture of appeal. 'Lucy love, I wasn't complaining. I wouldn't miss falling in with you for anything!' He laid one hand over his heart. 'Here I am, your willing slave for the night, your pleasure my pleasure.'

'A willing slave,' Buffy repeated, as though that was her idea of heaven, and if only Josh would offer such slavery to her she'd snap it up.

Things were definitely getting out of control here, Lucy thought, but didn't know what to do about it. She'd brought it upon herself, agreeing to Josh's plan, but now she wasn't sure it was leading to anywhere she wanted to be. If James started thinking she was using Josh as a toy-boy...

'I didn't know you had dominatrix tendencies, Buffy,' James drawled, an edgy note in his voice.

'What?' Clearly she was attempting a mental shake as she switched her attention to him, but her big amber eyes looked empty of any understanding as they appealed for him to explain himself.

Lucy's mind was reeling, too. *A dominatrix?* Was that how he was now seeing her...in tight leather gear with a whip in hand, forcing men to perform to her will? She almost died on the spot!

Buffy's blankness forced James to speak again. 'Never mind,' he said bruskly. 'What do you think of the band?' He gestured to the musicians on stage to redirect her attention.

'Oh!' She obediently looked and listened. 'They've got a good beat. Is this the band you think may do as well as Silverchair?'

James pursued the conversation with Buffy, much to Lucy's relief. She needed some breathing space to assess what had happened, to get her thoughts into some kind of order for handling the rest of the night which now stretched ahead, loaded with perilous double meanings to everything!

'He's hooked,' Josh whispered triumphantly.

She looked askance at him. 'He's taken the bait but he doesn't like it.'

'And doesn't that say something? No indifference there, Lucy love. The man is wriggling beautifully.'

'But I don't want him to think I'm a dominatrix.' She was horrified by the image. Even more so, because she had actually fantasised him being handcuffed to her bed! But that was only a mad dream borne out of frustration, she assured herself. She'd never really do it. What she dearly, truly wanted was utterly breath-taking mutual desire.

'Challenges his manhood,' Josh murmured knowingly. 'He'll be thinking about how much he'd like to dominate you.'

She frowned at him. 'Do you realise you've made yourself out to be my toy-boy?'

He grinned. 'So what? You think Buffy is anything more than a toy-girl to him? What's good for the goose is good for the gander. Makes you more of a match for him.'

She shook her head. 'I doubt he'll think that.'

'Give him time. He might not realise it yet but that guy is possessive of you, Lucy, and right now he's as jealous as hell of me. Why do you think he seated you next to him? To compete for your attention, that's why.'

Could it be so? Lucy found it difficult to believe, yet Josh was no fool in his perceptions of people. And the miserable truth was, James had never sought her company on a personal basis before. Outside of work, he'd been perfectly content with the Buffys of this world.

Until now.

All the same, company in public and company in private were still two different things. Josh could very well be right in that he'd hit some competitive nerve in James. However, that didn't mean she was actually desirable to him, not in the sense she craved. This was probably dog in the manger stuff. He didn't want her himself but he didn't like the idea of someone else having her.

Besides, what was the point in planting false images of her in his mind? What would it win her in the end? She wanted to be wanted for herself, not fancied as some kind of sexual contestant.

'I'm *me* and I'm not going to pretend to be anything else,' she stated emphatically.

'Neither you should,' Josh agreed. 'Being you is perfect.'

'Perfect for what?' she demanded suspiciously.

'Titillating him to death.' He gave her a smugly satisfied look. 'You did want him to burn, Lucy love. If nothing else, we have achieved that objective.'

True, she told herself.

Let him burn.

He'd made her burn all day.

Vengeance was sweet.

She could hand in her notice with the sense she'd had the last word with James Hancock. He'd be left thinking he'd missed out on something. And he had. She *was* worth more than the label of secretary.

CHAPTER FOUR

JAMES was not enjoying himself.

He couldn't fault the food served. It was gourmet standard. Yet he found himself irritated by the bits of decorative garnishes that were so artistically arranged on each plate. Pretentious garbage. He had a perverse desire for something plain and solid, like sausages and mash. But he made all the right noises, joining in the general chorus of approval.

Adding to his irritation was Buffy's vapid conversation. She was just like the gourmet food—pretty to look at, no substance. And her gaze kept sliding to Josh Rogan, who was clearly enjoying himself immensely, the life of the party, happily making everyone else happy, and dominating Lucy's attention.

Not that she hung on his every word. Surprisingly enough, she seemed to be her usual contained self, playing the straight woman to her lover's sparkle. Except on the dance-floor. She certainly wasn't *straight* there. She melted into the music, revealing a sensual suppleness that obviously reflected what she was like in bed, since she had a guy like Josh Rogan coming back for more and more whenever she wanted him.

She was a tantalising mix, and most irritating of

all was her prickly coolness to him. Each time he'd tried to engage her in conversation, she gave a few polite replies—the absolute minimum without being rude—then turned her attention to whatever else was being said around the table.

Paying him back for sitting her next to him, he'd concluded, her resentment at being reminded of work on her night off made very plain. It hadn't exactly been tactful of him to call her his punctilious secretary in front of everyone. He suspected it had put her off-side with him in more ways than one.

Even when he'd casually touched her she'd removed the contact as though he were a poisonous snake, a fierce rejection coming at him in tumultuous waves. Plus the accompanying look at Buffy, as if to say, 'There's your touchable doll. Paw her, not me, thank you.'

The more he thought about it, the more he decided Lucy Worthington was a control junkie. She remained on top of every situation at work. She had Josh Rogan on a string which she pulled in whenever it suited her. And she was very tight with money. In fact, the only time he'd ever seen her part with unnecessary dollars was when he'd hassled her into buying tickets in tonight's raffle—probably the first and only raffle tickets she'd ever bought.

'For the children, not the car,' she'd said, scorning his sales patter.

No doubt Lucy considered an Alpha Spider sports car a frivolous impracticality. Since she couldn't control the weather, a convertible would never be her pick for day-to-day travelling. If she chose to acquire a car at all, it would be a reliable hard-top with low fuel consumption.

James was sinking into a morose mood when one of the band members came to him, asking to have a private word. He quickly excused himself from the table, grateful to seize any diversion from the problem he had with Lucy. Besides, not involving her in any work-related issue demonstrated he was true to his word about leaving her free to enjoy herself tonight. Maybe she wouldn't be quite so prickly with him when he came back.

Lucy watched him go and hoped he'd never come back. He stirred so much tension in her, it was impossible to relax and enjoy herself. She took a long deep breath, trying to loosen up as she slowly released it, only to be then landed with Buffy Tanner who slid onto the chair James had vacated, determined on having a woman-to-woman chat.

'I love your boyfriend,' she purred into Lucy's ear. 'Where did you find such a gorgeous hunk?'

'Oh, I've known Josh for years,' she answered, not wanting to get specific.

'Why haven't you married him then?'

Lucy allowed herself a dry smile. 'That wouldn't suit either of us.'

Satisfaction oozed from Buffy. 'You mean he likes to stay free-wheeling.'

'We simply respect each other's life-style, Buffy.'

She nodded happily. 'I like that. James is such a

grump about punctuality. He doesn't make any concessions.'

'A flaw in paradise?'

'What?'

'I mean...everything isn't rosy in your relationship with James.'

She shrugged. 'Oh, he's so high-powered all the time. You must know what he's like, working for him. Always thinking about what's got to be done. Pressure, pressure, pressure.'

'Mmmh...that's probably what makes him successful.'

'I guess so.' Buffy didn't seem sure that success was worth so much attention. 'He is good at sex,' she added as though that was some compensation. Then leaning forward confidentially, 'I bet Josh is, too.'

'Mmmh,' Lucy agreed out of pride.

'Is he really built?'

'What?'

Buffy wrinkled her nose. 'You know. Some guys can have a great-looking physique, but when you get them down to the buff...very disappointing.'

Not knowing how to answer, Lucy blurted out, 'I take it James isn't disappointing.'

'Not in that area. He's big. And a real pistol. He can go on and on and on,' Buffy assured her, rolling her eyes appreciatively. 'What about Josh?'

Lucy took another deep breath, desperate to somehow get this conversation steered onto other ground. As it was, she didn't know how she was going to control her thoughts once James returned to his chair.

'Josh has never disappointed me,' she said truthfully, though the claim had nothing to do with sex. She turned curiously to Buffy. 'Do you always rate men on how they perform in bed?'

'Well, it is a big thing, isn't it?' Buffy reasoned. 'After all, it's what they want us for, so it's a dumb deal if *we* don't get satisfaction.'

'What about a sense of companionship? Enjoying other things together?'

'Huh! In my experience, men only put up with what I want to do, to get what's coming at the end of it. Sex is our bargaining chip, and I, for one, am not going to be a loser.'

Lucy had never thought of the relationship between men and women in such stark trading terms and it set her wondering how true Buffy's vision was. She didn't like it. She wanted to believe that one day she might have the best of both worlds, the kind of companionship she shared with Josh, plus the passionate sexual desire she wished she could share with James.

The band started playing again so whatever problem had arisen was apparently resolved. Her gaze fastened on James, striding back towards their table, and before she could stop the downward slide, she found herself staring at the movement of his thighs and thinking of what Buffy had said. Which so appalled her, a tide of heat burned up her neck and scorched her cheeks.

She snatched up her glass of champagne—assiduously re-filled by their waiter whenever the content lowered—and tried to bury her shame in it. Buffy, having also noticed James' approach, leapt to her feet, skirted Lucy's chair, and accosted Josh, leaning invitingly over his shoulder.

'Come dance with me, Josh. I can kidnap you from Lucy for one little dance, can't it?' she pressed with a pretty pout at both of them.

'Now that would be leaving my partner alone,' Josh chided charmingly.

'James is coming. He'll look after her,' Buffy quickly pointed out. 'He *loves* Lucy.'

'Well, should I or should I not stand in the path of true love?' he tossed at Lucy, his eyes dancing wickedly.

'Oh, go on. I'll manage,' she urged, wanting Buffy out of her hair before she said something awful in front of James, dragging her into even worse embarrassment.

'I am commanded,' Josh said, letting it be known it was not his preference before going off with Buffy, who didn't care as long as she was getting her own way. Though she was careful to avoid confronting James with her choice, deliberately not crossing paths with him as she led Josh to the dance-floor.

Of course, James noticed. He looked at them, looked at Lucy, and she felt herself bristling at what he probably thought—Buffy snagging the prize and Lucy left sitting like a shag on a rock. She glared defiantly at him as he pursued his own purposeful approach to the table.

His chair was still pushed back, where Buffy had left it, and instead of pulling it forward and sitting down, he stood in the empty space, making his close presence overwhelmingly felt. Lucy sipped some more champagne, doing her utmost to ignore him while every nerve in her body twanged with awareness.

'I see your partner has gone off with mine,' he remarked.

'Yes. Buffy was panting to dance with him so I let him indulge her.' That should set him back in his tracks, Lucy thought savagely.

'Will you indulge me?'

Her mind jammed, unable to follow his line of logic. She tried a lofty glance at him. 'I beg your pardon?'

His mouth curled into a wry smile, but his eyes were simmering with a very personal challenge. 'Would it be too much of a hardship for you to dance with me?'

Doubt and desire did a violent tango. 'If this is a courtesy…'

'It's not. I *want* to dance with you.'

Unable to believe it, Lucy expostulated, 'There's really no need to feel obliged…'

'I've wanted to dance with you all night,' he broke in, a note of ferocity in his voice. 'If you hadn't been so damned snappy at me, I would have asked you before this. Just say yes or no, Lucy. I'm not going to grovel.'

Grovel? The heat started a rush up her throat again at the reminder of the *dominatrix* tag. Compelled to deny both the idea he had of her, and the mess she was in at the thought of dancing with him, she pushed back her chair and stood up, driven to affirmative action.

'Let's dance,' she said with as much aplomb as she could muster.

His eyes flared with triumph as though he'd won a battle. He took her arm and tucked it around his, which was totally unnecessary for the short walk to the dance floor. Masterful, possessive...the words skidded wildly through Lucy's mind. Was Josh right? Had she suddenly become a sexual challenge to her boss?

It was just as well he had taken her arm because her legs turned to water at the thought of James Hancock actually lusting after an opportunity to show her what it would be like sharing a bed with him...all hot and hard and control-shattering, and never in a million years stooping to grovel for anything he wanted.

Her stomach contracted in a spasm of sheer nervous excitement. It was awful, reacting like this to the madness in her mind. It was even more awful when he whirled her onto the dance-floor, releasing her to start a face-to-face sequence of rock steps and she stumbled. Having frantically caught her balance and fiercely willed her legs to behave themselves, she tried to focus on the beat of the music, wanting to match his movements.

But it was so distracting watching him, the glide and stamp of his powerful legs, the sway of his snaky-lean hips, the bump and grind that seemed so overtly suggestive. She got hopelessly out of time, her own movements stiff and jerky, not in tune at all with what she should be doing.

'Now you just quit that right now, Lucy,' James growled at her, his expression thunderous.

'Quit what?' she babbled, utterly helpless to correct the havoc he stirred.

'This perverse resistance you're going on with.' He literally glowered with ferocity. 'I saw you dancing with Josh. Pretending you're some awkward amateur is a really petty insult.'

'I'm used to dancing with Josh,' she protested, hunting for some inoffensive excuse for being out of kilter. 'I'm comfortable with him. He's not my boss.'

'This is not the office,' he argued.

'You're still my boss,' she insisted.

His eyes flashed blue lightning. 'Time you stopped putting your life into neat little pockets. Forget playing safe. Take a risk.'

He caught her totally off-guard, grabbing her and hauling her in to him with a thump that left her breathless. Or maybe it was the impact of feeling a vital wall of muscle connected to her wobbly frame that stole her ability to breathe. His arms wound around her back, holding her intimately pinned to him. Her arms had nowhere to go except up on his shoulders and they just slid naturally around his neck.

'Now melt,' he commanded gruffly.

And Lucy melted.

Her breasts seemed glued to the heat of his chest. Her stomach quivered mushily with the awareness of what it was pressed against. Her thighs clung to the strength of his. And her feet...her feet followed his as though it was what they were born to do. The only thing that didn't melt was her heart. It was going nineteen to the dozen, super-energised by the volatile energy flowing from him.

'That's better,' he muttered, satisfaction coating his voice.

Lucy kept her mouth shut. It wasn't actually a conscious decision not to answer him. She was speechless as well as breathless at what was happening. James Hancock had her clamped in the kind of embrace she had dreamed about and there was nothing the least bit platonic about the way he was dancing with her. She was in seventh heaven.

She had no idea if this was some exhibition of macho manhood that demanded he get the better of her. Right at this moment, she didn't care. She was revelling in the sense of having him where she wanted him. Well, not exactly *where*, but it was close. It was certainly an exhilarating taste of the sexual power he exerted.

And he was not unmoved by her, either. She could definitely feel his arousal. Amazingly he didn't seem at all concerned about removing himself to a discreet distance. Was *he* revelling in feeling her pliant softness, imagining what it might be like to move what was currently outside her, *inside?*

That thought melted her even further, reducing her to a state of feverish mindlessness. Breathless, speechless, mindless, her treacherous body just kept on responding to wherever he led, circling the dance-floor as one, moving with a continually pressing sensuality, the physical friction becoming so acute, Lucy felt herself on the verge of climax.

The music stopped. It took Lucy a few moments to understand why James was no longer moving her around. Her ears finally registered that the band had finished playing. It struck her that, despite their mutual arousal, he had been more aware of external things than she had, which instantly cooled her brain.

Had he been on some sexual ego-trip, flagrantly demonstrating how much of a *pistol* he was...better than Josh? Lucy's excitement died on the spot. She started shrivelling away from the intimate contact, deeply relieved that he couldn't know how much he had affected her. Having unlocked her hands from the nape of his neck and got them as far as his shoulders, she found her attempt to extract herself from her boss thwarted by the tightening clamp of his arms.

'The band will start another number soon,' was his excuse.

Lucy took a deep breath, needing a full blast of

mind-clearing oxygen. She was *not* going to get carried away on a fantasy again. It was too shaming when she knew perfectly well it was Buffy Tanner he'd be going to bed with tonight.

'This dance is over,' she stated with frosty finality, pushing at his shoulders to make her intent clear.

He marginally loosened his embrace, enough for her to lean back and look him straight in the eyes. Which was a big mistake because the eyes that looked straight back into hers were smouldering with desire, confusing her sensible train of thought.

'Don't say you didn't enjoy it, Lucy,' he challenged.

She took another deep breath. 'You're a very good dancer, James,' she answered, wary of committing herself to anything more than that.

'We flowed together,' he insisted.

'Well, the music finally got to me,' she parried, proudly determined on not admitting anything else had got to her. Buffy was still in the wings. 'Now if you don't mind, the music has stopped and I would like my own space back.'

His eyes glittered. 'Because I'm your boss?'

Her chin tilted defiantly. 'That's one reason.'

'Are labels more important to you than people?'

'It was you who labelled me *your punctilious secretary*,' she flashed back at him.

'Which was very wrong of me and I apologise for it,' he said, sweeping that mat out from under her feet.

She struggled to keep it there, not knowing where

this was leading and feeling intensely vulnerable. 'I'm not your partner here tonight,' she blurted out.

'And if I said I wish you were…?'

Her mind went into another spin of doubt and desire. 'I think you must have drunk a lot of champagne.'

'Is it so impossible to think you could be the wine in my blood, Lucy?'

The eight months of non-interest blasted his contention. 'Since when, James?' she demanded sceptically. 'Since I turned up with Josh tonight? Did that titillate your fancy? Not so *boring* after all?'

'You have never bored me,' he declared vehemently.

'So you told me earlier. Me to entertain you, Buffy to satisfy your other needs,' she threw at him savagely. 'So let's just keep to the rules.'

Having hurled down that bitter gauntlet, she shoved herself out of his embrace, stepping back on trembling legs and swinging towards the stage where a man was announcing something over the microphone. She concentrated fiercely on grasping what was being said, determined on blocking James out until the violent turbulence he'd stirred could be brought under control.

'…and the winner is…Lucy Worthington…of Bellevue Hill, Sydney!'

Stunned at hearing her own name being blared out through the auditorium, Lucy couldn't apply any sense to it. Suddenly Josh burst through the crowd on the dance-floor, picked her up and whirled her

around, laughingly crowing, 'The Alpha Spider
sports car! It's yours, Lucy love! You've won it!'

The raffle!

The *wish* prize!

Miracles could happen to her, she thought dizzily.

And maybe—just maybe—if she threw the rules
away and acted like Buffy, another miracle could
happen!

CHAPTER FIVE

JAMES stood with his hands clenched, fighting the violent urge to rip Lucy away from Josh Rogan and smash his handsome face in. Never had he felt so aggressively possessive of a woman. The adrenaline pumping through him was priming every caveman instinct he had, adding to the problem of easing the hard-on that dancing with Lucy had aroused. He fiercely told himself he'd look an absolute fool if he tried any move at all.

Buffy slid out of the dance crowd and hugged his arm. 'How lucky can you get?' she exclaimed, heaving her lush breasts in a huge sigh of envy.

Having her rubbing against him should have been some consolation. It wasn't. The whole sum of Buffy's delectable femininity couldn't turn him on at this moment. In fact, it had the opposite effect. The discomfort Lucy had left him with was instantly lowered—from a rod to a turkey in no time flat.

'I'd love a car like that,' Buffy purred.

And a man like Josh Rogan, James thought viciously. Not that he cared about Buffy wanting Lucy's partner. She could have him. The sooner the better, detaching Josh from Lucy and freeing her of scruples about sticking to partners. Though James knew in his bones this wasn't going to happen. Josh was only too happy to be with Lucy, sweeping her up on stage to find out how to claim her prize.

The band started up again, a joyous jazzy number. There was no joy whatsoever in James as he resigned himself to dancing with Buffy. He wanted Lucy back in his arms. And she was totally wrong about him not fancying her before tonight. It was just that tonight the desires she'd been stirring had zoomed into flesh and blood reality...holding her, feeling her responding to him, the sheer sensual surrender she'd given him in their dance together.

Lucy unbuttoned...not yet in actuality, but he'd certainly got the sense of what she would be like when all her inhibitions—and clothes—were shed.

A series of highly erotic scenes occupied James' mind as he danced on with Buffy. He'd been left in little doubt that sticking to partners was the order tonight, but come Monday, when he had Lucy to himself in the office, the rules were going to change. She couldn't put Josh Rogan between them then. Nor Buffy. And if she arrived all buttoned up tight in her secretary role...well, he'd take great pleasure in probing for button-holes.

Lucy was riding high on a rainbow of delight. She'd won a pot of gold with the Alpha Spider sports car. Of course, she wouldn't get the full value of the flashy red convertible when she sold it back to the dealer, but she would still be able to pay a huge chunk off her mortgage on the apartment, as well as buy the furniture she wanted.

'I still can't believe my luck! You'd better pinch me, Josh,' she whispered as they left the official who'd explained how the prize could be collected.

He laughed. 'You're definitely on a winning streak.' Cocking a wicked eyebrow, he added, 'Seemed to me the course of true love was running hot as you danced with your boss.'

She grimaced. 'Hardly true love.'

'Lust unlimited?'

'There are limits on the dance-floor, but it was...'

'Stimulating?'

'Mmmh...'

'Never underestimate chemistry.'

The dance-floor had emptied. As they crossed it towards their table, Lucy looked nervously for James, secretly hoping Josh was right about chemistry, though she couldn't help doubting the factors that had stirred it tonight. Would she be making a fool of herself if she did give out some encouraging signals?

Maybe she shouldn't hand in her resignation. Maybe she should wait and see if something real developed between James and herself, not just a flash in the pan fancy, brought on by unusual circumstances. If she was still the wine in his blood in the cold light of day in the office...Lucy heaved a fluttery sigh. Hope certainly had a way of worming through a whole thicket of thorny doubts.

Her heart skittered all over the place when James turned in his chair and smiled warmly at her as Josh saw her seated. 'Congratulations!' he rolled out with every appearance of pleasure in her winning luck.

'I'm sick with envy,' Buffy declared, 'but it's fantastic for you, Lucy. You must be tripping on Cloud Nine.'

'I am,' Lucy happily admitted, flicking an appreciative look at James. 'Thank you.'

'Here comes the red terror on the highway,' one of the other men joked.

It spurred a string of light-hearted comments around the table.

'You'll have to be careful of police patrols. A sports convertible is like flashing up a speed sign to them.'

'Great fun driving one though.'

'And you'll be fighting guys off with a stick. You'll have to watch out, Josh.'

'The sun in your face, wind in your hair...heaven on wheels.'

James laughed and shook his head. 'I'll bet right now none of that will happen.'

'Why not?' Buffy demanded.

'Because Lucy will never drive that car.' He looked knowingly at her. 'She'll make a deal with the dealer and take the money.'

It was precisely what she had planned, but hearing James say it with such smug confidence had the perverse effect of making her want to deny it. 'Why do you think so?' she demanded, her hackles rising over the *boring* image again.

His eyes filled with amused mockery. 'Because it's the sensible thing to do.'

Sensible! She seethed over the word, despite how true it was of her.

'And you are always very sensible about money, Lucy,' he added, rubbing it in. 'You never do anything extravagant.'

That was even more true, she had to concede, but it was a truth she suddenly wanted to blow to bits, and to hell with being sensible! She wanted to wear outrageously sexy clothes like Buffy. She wanted to whiz around in a red sports convertible with the wind in her hair. She wanted to seize the pleasures of the day and forget about tomorrow. She wanted to rock James Hancock so far off his feet with her *unpredictability* he wouldn't know if he was coming or going with her.

'I'll be taking Monday off, James,' she stated recklessly.

He frowned, not liking this turn of events. 'What for?' he demanded.

'I can claim my car on Monday and that's exactly what I'm going to do,' she went on, hurling common sense to the winds.

'You're taking it?' His voice rose incredulously.

The tone of utter disbelief was music to Lucy's ears. James Hancock could just pull her right out of the pigeon-hole he'd put her in and think again!

'I hope it won't inconvenience you too much,' she said sweetly, 'but I do need the time off. Of course, I won't expect you to pay me for the day...'

His eyebrows beetled down. 'I'm not that mean, Lucy.'

She smiled. 'I can be quite extravagant when I choose to be, James. I don't mind...'

'Don't be absurd,' he cut in tersely. 'You've never even taken a sick day off.'

Her smile tilted into irony. 'It's my curse to be healthy.'

'And I'm very grateful for it. You're entitled to a free day on full pay. It's nonsense to suggest otherwise.'

'As you wish,' she conceded, feeling an exhilarating zing of triumph at having flouted his picture of her and extracted what she wanted from him.

'Can you drive?' he shot at her.

Lucy bristled. Did he think her so stodgy and narrow in the life she lived, that handling a car had never entered into it? She ungritted her teeth enough to say, 'Like most people, James, I got my driving licence in my teens.'

'Handling a sports car is a bit different to driving a sedate sedan.'

Sedate! Lucy's teeth ground together again. She'd show him, she thought wildly. His worthy Miss Worthington was going to be the most unsedate secretary he'd ever seen, come Tuesday morning.

'I think I'd better take Monday off, too, and come with you when you take possession of the car,' he went on, frowning over her possible incompetence. 'Run you through its paces so you can feel secure with it.'

Secure! He was hitting all the buttons that made her so unexciting! 'That's not necessary,' she grated.

'Lucy...' He looked earnestly at her. 'It's often inexperience that causes accidents. I care about you.'

Did he? Did he really? Or was he worried about having to do without his secretary if she smashed herself up?

'You could underestimate the power, the acceleration,' he explained. 'And because you're lower to the ground in a sports car, the road will feel different, look different.'

'James does know,' Buffy put in helpfully. 'He drives a Porsche.'

Such wonderful common sense, Lucy thought bitterly, and common sense had nothing to do with all the things she planned to do between now and Tuesday morning. While it was nice of James to offer help with the car—condescendingly nice—she didn't want to be in his company again until she was good and ready. There was one way to squash this whole idea and she took it.

'Josh drives an MG,' she told Buffy, then turned to James. 'It's very kind of you to offer your services, but I truly don't need them. I'll be fine, thank you.'

He looked put out, his mouth tightening, his jaw jutting, his eyes momentarily flashing a savage glitter as he said, 'Then I can confidently expect you in the office on Tuesday morning.'

'No problem,' she assured him, though she

fiercely hoped she'd be giving him a lot of problems when she arrived.

'James took me to the MG Restaurant where they have those cars on display,' Buffy told Josh. 'They looked fabulous.'

'Mine is a much older vintage,' he dryly informed her. 'A fifties model which I've restored to its former glory.'

This sparked interest around the table and Lucy relaxed, glad the spotlight was now off her. Having embraced madness, she started plotting her moves for the next three days. The car was a windfall anyway, she argued rebelliously to the thrifty voice inside her head, and it wouldn't break her to buy a few new clothes. The furniture could wait. The payments on her mortgage would simply stay the same.

But what about the cost of car registration?

Insurance?

Fuel?

Parking fees?

Stop it! she commanded. If James Hancock could be won with these tactics, she was going to do it, no matter what. A woman was entitled to one period of madness in her life. She might be dead next week. Seize the day. No shilly-shallying. Just go for it!

James sat in seething silence as the rest of the party carried on about vintage cars. Lucy's determination to hold him at arm's length was extremely frustrating. Even out of the office on her day off, it was no go. She had him pigeon-holed as her boss and there he was going to stay, despite the indications of what they could have together. And the deceptive image she had carried off all these months had clearly been designed to put him off, too.

Not that it had completely fooled him. His instincts had been aware there was more to Lucy Worthington than met the eye. Her *real* life was spilling out tonight.

He turned to her, suspicion wanting proof. 'You wore this standby little black dress tonight because I'm here,' he stated bluntly.

She looked startled. 'I beg your pardon.'

'It's a *work* dress, isn't it? And that's your *work* hair-do, too.'

She affected bewilderment. 'I'm sorry if you think I'm inappropriately dressed.'

'Not at all. I'm just working you out, Lucy Worthington. It's been quite an enlightening night,' he declared tauntingly.

Her face lit with a smile that seemed to say he hadn't even scratched the surface of her. She reached out, picked up her glass of champagne, and raised it in a toast. 'Well, here's to better days!'

And nights, James darkly vowed, as he echoed the toast with mocking grace and drank with her. If it was the last thing he did, he'd find out all there was to know of Lucy Worthington. Every intimate detail! Monday was now a write-off, but come Tuesday…if he had to shake her out of her buttons, he would.

CHAPTER SIX

NOT even the coolness of the night lowered the fever in Lucy's brain. The ball was over but her feet still felt like dancing as she and Josh walked from the convention centre to the parking station. She had hooked James Hancock's interest. No doubt about it now. The trick was to pull out all stops to hold it engaged.

'What are you going to tell your mother?' Josh asked, a curious lilt in his voice.

'Mum?'

A spear of guilt pierced Lucy's intoxicating dreams of conquest and triumph. Her mother wouldn't approve these wild and wanton plans at all. In fact, she'd have a pink fit if she even heard a whisper of them.

'I'm not going to tell her anything,' she said decisively, and cast Josh a stern look. 'And don't you dare gossip to your mother, either. You know they belong to the same Businesswomen's Association.'

He held up both hands in a gesture of innocence. 'Mum's the word. Your secrets are my secrets, Lucy love.'

'Good! Just keep them that way,' she insisted.

Josh and his mother were close, invariably telling each other everything. In fact, Lucy had often envied the very open loving relationship they shared. Sally Rogan was a warm, happy person. Widowed when Josh was only three, she had opened a fashion boutique which was a thriving business because she'd always taken the time to chat to her customers and get to know what appealed to them.

Her own mother tended to preach to her customers. She ran a health food shop and styled herself as an authority on what was good for everyone. In personality, Ruth Worthington and Sally Rogan were chalk and cheese. Being sensible came first with Ruth, while having fun came first with Sally.

The two women didn't mix in any social sense, though they'd both lived and worked in the same town for over thirty years. Being in business was the only thing they had in common, and when they went to those meetings they were usually polite to each other, prompted, no doubt, by the long-term friendship between Josh and Lucy, which also occasionally led to the swapping of family news. Tonight's news had to be kept off that agenda at all costs.

Lucy knew what she would be in for if it wasn't. Her mother didn't approve of extravagance and didn't know the meaning of fun. Or she'd lost all sense of it when her husband had left her for another woman. Lucy had no memory of a father. He'd gone before she was two years old, but she'd been drilled in lessons from that desertion for as long as she could remember.

You can't count on men to look after you.

Make your own security.

Never lose your head over a man. He'll take advantage of you.

And so on, and so on, and so on.

Now bent on breaking just about all of those rules, Lucy didn't want any accusing lectures from her mother. She'd suffer her own grief from this decision if she had to, but inviting a battering stream of 'I told you so's' would only add misery to misery if nothing worked out as she wanted it to.

'So how are you going to hide the car?' Josh quizzed.

She heaved a sigh, knowing full well what her mother would say about running a red sports convertible. 'I'll keep it in Sydney.'

'You're still going to catch the train to Gosford every time you visit your mother?'

'Easier than flaunting that extravagance in her face. It would be like waving a red rag at a bull. Besides, it's not as if it's a long train trip.'

In fact, it was only an hour and ten minutes on the fast northbound trains between Sydney and Gosford. She usually read a book, which she couldn't do driving a car—one of the reasons she preferred public transport. Lucy had never found it a hardship to do without her own vehicle.

'Waste of a great car, not using it on the expressway,' Josh remarked. 'You should let yourself enjoy it and to hell with what your mother thinks.'

'I will enjoy it. But I'll probably end up selling it so why cause a hassle?'

'Ah!'

The 'Ah!' was so full of understanding, Lucy blushed. 'You said I should be unpredictable,' she reminded him.

Josh laughed and started singing, *'This is the moment...'*

She laughed, too, her tingling feet performing a pirouette as she threw out her arms and exultantly sang *'This is the time...'*

Josh caught her waist and lifted her up to the stars—metaphorically speaking—and they laughed in a mad, joyous celebration of victory over the frustration that had originally driven Lucy this evening. Miracles were definitely in the air.

'Well, Lucy love, if you're really going to *show* him you'll have to let your hair down,' Josh merrily advised as he set her on her feet again.

'I intend to.'

'Some shopping is in order.'

'Will you help me, Josh? Do you have some spare time tomorrow? I want some really modern sexy stuff to go with the convertible but I don't want to look too tarty.'

'We'll trawl the streets tomorrow afternoon,' he promised.

'Great!' She hugged his arm as they proceeded into the parking station. 'You've got such a good fashion eye. I'm bound to choose the wrong things.'

'Flattery will get you everywhere.'

'You're the best friend!'

He patted her hand with indulgent affection. 'Lucy love, it will be a huge pleasure to see the butterfly emerge from your mother's narrow little cocoon.'

She frowned. 'Have I been so stodgy?'

'Not stodgy. Never stodgy,' he assured her. 'But to a large extent you have lived by the constraints your mother put on you. If you get too fixated on being *safe*, you miss out on much of the fun in life, and you never live life to the full.'

But you don't fall down a hole, Lucy argued to herself, then realised her thought was parroting what her mother said. She shook her head, disturbed by the idea she was living a brain-washed life instead of a life of her own.

'Take the suits you wear to work,' Josh went on seriously. 'They armour you against risk. They're safe, beyond criticism, properly professional, but they don't express the real Lucy. Not the Lucy I know. They're a reflection of your mother.'

'I guess they are,' she answered thoughtfully.

'Nothing exciting about wearing those clothes.'

'That's true. I just bung them on and go.'

'It shouldn't be like that, Lucy. You should love the clothes you wear.'

She gave him an arch look. 'This is *your* mother talking now.'

'Mum's right. Clothes should lift your spirits, make you feel good about yourself. The attitude of *this will do*, is an expression of compromise, accepting you're not worth more. It's a downer. You should never do that to yourself.'

'Well, I'll let you have your way with me tomorrow,' she declared, feeling she had let herself down in this area.

'Not *my* way. *Your* way.'

'But I might get it wrong.'

He shook his head. 'It will be in the smile on your face, the zing in your heart. The right clothes for the person you are do that for you. All you have to do is go with that flow. Trust it and don't let anyone else's opinion spoil it.'

Lucy took a deep breath and resolved to be boldly free, choosing whatever thrilled her and made her feel sexy. No more *work* clothes. No more *work* hair-do. She grinned at the thought of James trying to work out the new Lucy Worthington when she presented her on Tuesday morning.

Having arrived at the parking slot where they had left the MG, Josh steered her to the driver's side. 'Better get in some practice,' he pressed.

Lucy baulked. 'I can't drive your pride and joy.'

'To my knowledge, the only car you've driven is your mother's Ford with automatic gears. James Hancock had one thing right tonight. A sports car is different.' He opened the door. 'Get in. I'll give you a lesson.'

'But what if I dent it or something getting out of this parking station?' she fretted.

He gave her a devil-may-care grin. 'I'll take the risk.'

The dancing challenge in his eyes spurred her on. After all, it was what she'd determined to do...*take the risk.* She stepped into the MG and settled herself in the driver's seat. Her hands curled around the wheel.

This is it, she told herself.

I'm going for it.

Starting now.

By Tuesday morning she'd be on a roll and James Hancock wouldn't know what hit him. It was a delicious thought.

'Right. Give it some juice,' Josh instructed, having settled beside her.

She giggled and switched on the ignition.

Juicy Lucy...

Starting now.

CHAPTER SEVEN

WITH a spring in his step, a smile hovering on his lips, and a lively sense of anticipation tingling through the rest of him, James opened the door to his secretary's office, fully expecting to find Lucy at work preparing for his arrival. It was instantly deflating to see no sign of her.

He checked his watch—five minutes short of nine o'clock. She wasn't exactly late, yet she invariably came in earlier than this. He'd never known her not be here before him. Her failure to do so on *this* Tuesday morning was aggravating, particularly since he'd given her Monday off.

As it was, he'd hardly done any work yesterday, distracted by her absence from the office and the gnawing desire to move their relationship onto new ground. Despite telling himself over and over again it was stupid to mess with what had been an ideal working partnership, he couldn't block out the temptation that had been raging through him since Friday night.

He *wanted* Lucy Worthington.

He hadn't even stayed with Buffy after the ball. Nor had he felt the slightest spark of interest in any of the women at the party he'd attended on Saturday night. There was only one woman he wanted to be with and she was frustrating him again right now.

A hopeful thought struck. He strode across her office and opened the connecting door to his. She wasn't there, either. Feeling doubly vexed, James didn't even think of settling to work without Lucy. He walked over to her desk and propped himself against it, arms folded in displeasure, ready to confront her with her tardiness when she did arrive.

There was no excuse for it. Getting from Bellevue Hill to this office building in Woolloomooloo presented no real difficulty. She didn't have to drive through inner-city traffic and Lucy wasn't ignorant of how to get into the basement car-park. She'd been a passenger in his car many times. He was not going to be drawn into worrying about the possibility of an accident. A woman in as much control of her life as Lucy Worthington was, did not have accidents.

Everything seemed unnaturally quiet, now that the other offices on this floor had been vacated and the company of solicitors that had taken them over wouldn't be moving in until next week. He had no client appointments this morning so there was only Lucy to come—Lucy to break the loneliness that had so irked him yesterday.

The hurried clack of heels on the tiled corridor leading from the elevators, momentarily straightened him up. Aware that his body was suddenly buzzing with tension, James forced himself to relax against the desk again. He was not going to look eager for Lucy's arrival. He was the boss here, not a lap-dog panting for his mistress's attention. The situation could get completely out of hand if he didn't remain master of it.

A woman whirled into the office, closing the door he'd left open, arrogantly assuming the right to seal off privacy. Annoyed by the unwelcome intrusion, James snapped upright again. A few terse words were about to spill off his tongue when the woman swung around and froze, shocked at being directly faced with his unexpected presence.

'James!' His name hissed out on a long, shaky breath.

Lucy?

Stunned disbelief rendered him speechless. A wealth of shiny brown hair swirled around her shoulders, wisps of it flying out as though electric from being in the wind. Her face was vibrant with colour...glowing cheeks, glossy red lipstick and sparkling green eyes. Quite clearly green, and fringed by long dark lashes. She wasn't wearing spectacles!

And what she *was* wearing hit him like a punch in the gut, taking his breath away. The clingy lime-green singlet top was a *long* way from conservative. Not only did the bold colour leap out at him, but so did her breasts, the stretchy material outlining them perfectly. Small breasts compared to Buffy Tanner's but firmly rounded and delectably tip-tilted at him— no sag anywhere, sideways or downwards—and she certainly wasn't wearing a bra to aid their shape.

Much, much better without one. No aid needed at all.

Floating between the provocative peaks was an embroidered butterfly—its wings a neon glow of violet and red and green. And it wasn't the only butterfly. Her skirt was printed with them—a virtual kaleidoscope of brilliant butterflies on a white background, flying every which way. It was a short straight little skirt—shorter than anything Lucy had ever worn before—hugging her hips and ending mid-thigh, with a couple of rows of frivolous little frills around the hem, giving a swinging effect that was very cutely sexy.

Her legs were bare—more leg than he'd ever seen on his secretary—and proof positive that they were, indeed, very shapely. On her feet she wore what looked like ballet slippers, with straps crossed over around her ankles, but they weren't black. They were lime-green.

James had the mad thought that she had danced all the way to the office, twirling around in that provocative little skirt, and ruffling her long hair into loose havoc, swinging the silky-looking lime-green bag she was carrying. Not a proper, clipped up leather hand-bag, a more casual, open-topped, cloth one.

No buttons in sight anywhere!

His heart started hammering. This had to be the *real* Lucy Worthington. And was she *something!* To think she'd been right under his nose all along, hiding her true self from him, wasting time that could have been spent exploring the full potential of a relationship between them.

Resentment at her duplicity fired every aggressive male hormone in his body. No more pulling the wool over his eyes. He had her in his sights now and he wouldn't be content until she was his in every sense there was.

'I'm sorry if I've kept you waiting,' she rushed out.

The tantalising little witch had kept him waiting eight months for this!

'I got into the wrong traffic lane,' she babbled on, 'and ended up being forced to go through the harbour tunnel, then on to North Sydney before I could turn around and come back over the bridge.'

She heaved a sigh that fixed his gaze on her breasts again. Buttons there, underneath the stretchy fabric, pushing it out, two perky buttons that blatantly invited a tug of his teeth.

'I'm just not used to driving in city peak hour.'

James dragged his gaze up from her peaks—reluctantly past her crushed-strawberry red mouth—to the glistening appeal in her eyes. Fantastic green eyes. Those bland spectacles had blurred their impact. Deliberately, no doubt. So why was she showing them now? Good question!

His mind belatedly clicked onto the excuse she'd been offering for her lateness. 'Takes experience,' he agreed sympathetically, needing to slide into probing her motives.

'I won't make the same mistake again,' she assured him.

'No problem.' He made an airy gesture, forgiving her confusion on the road, his mind busily occupied with finding the best way through her formidable defences.

She frowned reflectively. 'You know, I think it's the red sports car. It seems to spur other drivers into being aggressive. Like they want to block it in or beat it.'

While getting as much as an eyeful of you as they can, James thought.

With a very sexy shrug, she added, 'Anyhow, it was really hair-raising out there this morning.'

'So I notice,' he said dryly, his gaze flicking to the long wild tresses.

'Oh!' She lifted an arm and attempted to pat down the wayward strands. 'Guess I'm a bit wind-blown. I'll tidy up shortly.'

'Don't on my account.' He smiled, feeling like a shark on the prowl all primed to bite into a tasty morsel...the lifted breast, the soft underarm... 'I like the new image,' he said, laying the obvious on the line for her to pick up and explain.

She blushed, then instantly took evasive action as though suddenly aware of having raised attention that might prove uncomfortable. 'Blame Orlando for that,' she tossed off as with quick purposeful steps she skirted him to get around behind her desk.

He swung to keep her in sight, grimly digesting this new unpalatable information. 'Orlando? You've thrown Josh over for some other guy?' he quizzed, his eyes mocking her fickleness as his stomach clenched at the thought of more competition to get rid of.

'No.' She dumped her bag on her chair and faced him with a look of defiant pride. 'Josh will always be…special. We understand each other.'

'I take it he understands Orlando,' he retorted sardonically, unable to believe that any man would like sharing Lucy with other lovers.

'Yes, he does.' A smile tugged at her mouth. 'I christened the car Orlando.'

James blinked. 'The car?'

'Calling it an Alpha Spider seemed all wrong to me. Spiders are creepy-crawly.' She shuddered expressively before breaking into a full-blown grin. 'The dealer said owning an Alpha was like having an Italian love affair and the name flashed straight into my mind…Orlando…' She drawled it seductively.

James laughed in sheer relief. This he could understand. She'd fallen in love with the car. He relaxed, hitching himself onto her desk, feeling more the master of the situation than he had before. Lucy was here with him, showing herself in her true colours, and he could proceed to pin the butterfly down.

'I take it you're now dressing for Orlando, the thrill of doing so having suddenly become more important to you than continuing your secretary role.'

She looked at him uncertainly. 'I'm still your secretary...aren't I? I mean...you don't actually *need* me to dress...'

'Like a prim spinster?'

She blushed again, no doubt inwardly squirming at his accurate description.

'No, I don't need that, Lucy,' he went on, enjoying the sense of being on top. 'I never did need it. I'm just wondering why you did it. After all, my business is *show* business.'

The green eyes flashed with some indecipherable but strong emotion. 'Considering the people you deal with, James, I thought you'd be more comfortable with a contrast.'

'Ah, thinking of my comfort, were you?'

Her chin tilted. 'I think you found it very comfortable, having the *worthy* Miss Worthington—' a scathing edge there '—be your ready handmaiden.'

The knives were out! A buzz of exhilaration zipped through James. Office hours had often been enlivened by verbal duels with Lucy, but this one was slicing open fascinating territory.

'All an act for my benefit, was it?' he challenged.

'No. It suited me, as well. I've simply shifted my priorities,' she declared.

'No longer caring about my comfort zone.'

'I didn't notice you caring about my comfort zone on Friday night,' she flashed back at him.

'Ah! The plot thickens. It's not entirely Orlando pressing your buttons.' He slid off her desk, impelled to prove what he was saying. The memory of how she'd melted in his arms brought an exciting wave of confidence. 'I got under your skin, didn't I? A little payback, Lucy?'

Her eyes simmered with a wealth of feeling. 'Why shouldn't I do what I want to do?' she hotly retorted.

'You should,' he agreed silkily. 'You very definitely should.'

As he rounded the desk, she gripped the back of her chair as though to stop herself retreating. The tension flowing from her was electric, pumping his excitement higher. She stood her ground, tossing her head like a cornered thoroughbred, her nostrils flaring rebellion, eyes daring him to cross her space.

'It's not a payback,' she proudly insisted. 'I simply decided to please myself.'

'Fine! You please me, too.'

She took a deep breath. Her breasts lifted, luring him on. James knew he was probably suffering a major rush of blood to the head, but the need to catch this butterfly woman in his net before she took flight was overpowering.

She wrenched her gaze off him and flicked an agitated glance at the filing cabinet. 'Is there something urgent you need for work?'

'You expect me to think of work with you dressed like this, Lucy?'

Her eyes flashed back to him, glittering with counter-challenge. 'You told me yourself it was time to stop putting my life into little pockets.'

'And I was right. It's a major crime to fold such glorious hair into a pinned up pocket. It should flow free.' He reached out, lifting the long fall of hair from her left shoulder and trailing it through his outspread fingers...sensual silk.

She didn't make the slightest move. No protest, either verbal or physical. It was as though she was holding her breath, she was so still. There was no shock/horror in her eyes, more a mesmerised wonder, and the wild urges thrumming through James received a huge kick of encouragement. She *had* melted in his arms. Was everything within her poised to feel the same sensations again?

He had to know.

His gaze dropped to her mouth. Her lips were slightly parted, soft and red and glossy, as though moistened with the juice of berries. His arms moved instinctively, winding around her, pulling her close, pinning her to him as he tasted what he was driven to taste, and she gave her mouth to him, willingly, passionately as he plundered the sweetness within. No holding back. Her hands were around his head, pressing him on, eager, demanding, expressing an urgency that was wild for satisfaction.

All the erotic thoughts he'd had about Lucy raged through his mind. He remembered the temptingly pert jut of her bottom and ran his hands over it, wanting to squeeze the fullness of her cheeks. But the fabric of her skirt was stiff, not soft and giving. He hauled it up. Naked flesh...*naked!* No panties? Yes, a G-string dipping down the cleft. Nothing to get in the way, though, and he revelled in the lovely bare curves, cupping them, lifting them to fit her more closely to the rampant hardness stirred by her readiness to come his way.

Her way, too. No doubt about that.

She wriggled against him. Seductively. And her mouth was in a stormy tangle with his, both of them simulating what they really wanted, the excitement intense. She was on heat, definitely melting for him, except for the hard nubs pressing against his chest, more intoxicating proof of her arousal.

Buttons, he thought, and the desire to undo them shot through him, moving his hands to the sexy stretchy top she wore, shoving it up, pushing it over the mounds of her breasts, sliding a palm over them, rubbing the marvellous protrusions, so tight, bigger than he'd anticipated, big aureoles, too, feeling the different skin texture of them.

He had to look, had to see.

He wrenched his mouth from the hot intimacy of hers, grabbed a great hank of her gorgeous long hair and bent her back from him. Perfect, perfect breasts, the aureoles gleaming like ripe plums, and in the centre of them, such long nipples drawing him towards them. Irresistible.

He scooped Lucy off her feet, sliding her body up his until he could take one of the provocative peaks in his mouth, tugging at it with a greed he'd never felt before. She gave a throaty animal cry and the sheer wanton need he heard in it drove him to her other breast, and the hands in his hair, kneading, clutching, pushing, were telling him yes, yes, more,

more…but his body was screaming for its own satisfaction.

The desk. He'd fantasised having her there. His legs instantly chose to move to the end of it and he laid her down along the top, her hair sprawling out in a picture of glorious abandonment, her breasts thrust up to him, still irresistible. He leaned over and gave them his avid attention as he unfastened his trousers and unleashed his own needy flesh.

Already positioned between her thighs, her supple legs wound around his hips, ready to pull him into her, James paused only long enough to push the flimsy G-string aside. He could feel her urgent desire, hot, moist, quivery, and he plunged himself forward, travelling fast to the innermost depths of her, exulting in the convulsive welcome she gave him, the arch of her back as she lifted herself to take all he could give…sheer ecstacy, her coming instant, wine in his blood.

A moan of almost agonised bliss erupted from her throat as it arched, as well, making her hair ripple and swirl.

He rocketed out of control, pumping in a frenzy of exultation as she came again and again and again, crying out for more—'Yes, yes, yes…' her head writhing, her body writhing, the hot voluptuous flow of her making him feel like a king amongst men, riding triumphant, and she lay in front of him, his prize, surrendering all she was to his power.

His climax burst from him like a fountain of exquisite pleasure, and she arched once more, feeling it, wanting it, loving it.

She was beautiful, incredible, magnificent. While still revelling in the honeyed heat of their intimacy, he leaned over and kissed her breasts, wanting to capture the throb of her heart, the whole inner life of her beating for him, with him.

The peaks were still aroused, wonderfully sensitive to his caressing, but her legs had fallen limp, sliding down the back of his thighs. Knowing their connection couldn't last, he gathered her up in his arms and joined his mouth to hers, savouring her response to their kissing and holding her close, soothing her tremors as separation inevitably came.

But it had been great—totally mind-blowing—and as he ended their kiss, a grin of sheer happiness spread across his face and his joy bubbled into words.

'Now that, my dear Lucy, is the way to start a day!'

CHAPTER EIGHT

THE WAY to start a day?

Lucy couldn't believe her ears. She'd just been through the most body-shattering, mind-ravaging, heart-drumming, out of this world experience, and James marked it down as *the way to start a day?*

Like any old day?

Nothing special at all?

A quick fix in the morning to get him happily through his work hours?

Somehow she mustered the strength to lift her eyelashes enough for her to see his face while still veiling any tell-tale expression he might seize on for making some other crass comment.

He was beaming with the kind of elated energy one associated with winning a million-dollar jackpot in a lottery. Macho male scooping the pool. Lucy's mind went clickety-click through a series of thoughts that raised her sense of vulnerability to an all-time high.

He'd had her.

She'd fallen to him.

Game over.

He'd won.

She was just another woman who'd provided him with a kick-start to the day.

Never mind that the desire had been every bit as mutual as she had craved, Lucy's heart was wounded and her pride unbearably stung. A vengeful rebellion surged across her mind, firing up a drive to puncture *his* pride. And his smugly male satisfaction in having done what he wanted with her also needed to be dealt with.

'Is that *it?*' she asked, the need to shame him clawing through her.

He looked startled, astonished. His beaming face tightened up. His eyes narrowed into piercing challenge. 'Don't tell me *you* didn't get off on it, Lucy.'

'Oh, I did. It was great!' she conceded dismissively, hating him for reminding her how *easy* she'd been. An absolute pushover. She picked her hands off his shoulders and rolled her stretchy top back over her breasts, settling it down to her waist in a clear demonstration she was not on offer any more.

Her mind furiously sought ways to take the edge off his triumph. She was sitting on the edge of the desk. He was still standing between her legs and her skirt was crumpled against him, hiding his vital parts, but the unzipped zipper sparked wicked inspiration—a reason for being so easy for him. Words tripped out before she could have second thoughts.

'Buffy told me...'

No, she couldn't say it. She hated anyone being reduced to a lump of meat. It was wrong. Even though he considered her his *starter* for the day, retaliating in kind was beneath her.

'What did Buffy tell you?'

'Oh, nothing. It was just woman stuff,' she quickly excused.

His expression relaxed into smug indulgence. Probably priding himself on what a great lover he was, serving Buffy on Friday night, her this morning—and no doubt Buffy had told him he was great, too! A violent jealousy erupted in Lucy.

'You and Buffy were talking woman stuff?' he commented, obviously amused by his two women connecting.

If he went back to Buffy tonight…she couldn't bear it. The come-hither model was just using him. The way she'd gone after Josh, she certainly wasn't in love with James. She just liked having what he could give her, especially in the sex department, while Lucy yearned for much more.

'Like what?' he prompted, curiosity dancing with amusement.

Could she say it? Would he see how shallow his relationship with Buffy was?

'Come on, Lucy. Out with it,' he pressed. 'I want to know what you two found in common.'

You…but not after this, she thought vehemently. She would not be the starter of the day and let Buffy be the finisher. She would do the finishing herself. Right now!

'Buffy told me you had a big…' She still couldn't say it.

'A big what?'

Why was she hesitating? It would re-arrange his

thinking, wouldn't it? Make him see how crass he'd been. Buffy, too, in labelling him like that.

'That you're really built…where it counted to her,' she blurted out.

'What?'

He looked utterly floored. Some protective instinct rose to the fore and he hastily achieved a respectable appearance, his face quite red as he tucked himself under cover—red from embarrassment or anger she couldn't tell until he raised savagely glittering eyes.

'She discussed me with you…in those terms?' he growled.

Definitely anger.

Goodbye, Buffy, Lucy thought, feeling no regret whatsoever at ruining the other woman's playground. Besides which, if James had only been using the swimsuit model for sex, he deserved to have that smacked in his face. He probably thought of Buffy in similar terms—big boobs. At least, he couldn't think about her like that.

'Some women do talk about their lovers,' she explained, furiously justifying what she'd done, though beginning to feel agitated about it. She smoothed her skirt over her thighs, nervously needing more respectability herself. 'Buffy considers *big* important,' she explained further.

His eyebrows beetled down. 'Do you?'

Desperately hoping he felt more than an impulsive lust for her, she earnestly declared, 'I consider lots of things important, James.'

'I'm glad to hear it,' he said grimly. 'Though apparently you didn't mind hearing intimate details about me.'

'I didn't ask for them,' she defended.

Seething disbelief glared back at her.

Her heart jiggled uncertainly. Somehow this was all rebounding on her, making everything tacky. She didn't know how to extract herself from it. The truth spilled off her tongue.

'Buffy offered them, wanting to dig out details about Josh, if you must know.'

His eyes glittered. 'Did she get *his* details?'

'No, she didn't. I really don't think of people like that,' she strongly asserted.

'But you have been thinking of me like that or it wouldn't be still in your mind right now,' he retorted fiercely. 'What else did she say about me?'

It was getting worse, not better. She desperately wished she hadn't started this. Jealousy was a terrible thing. She shook her head in shame. 'I'm sorry. Please…can we just let this go?'

She slid off the desk, onto her feet, intending to side-step away from him.

His hands clamped on her shoulders, halting her attempt at escape. 'Tell me!' he commanded.

'I must go and tidy up. Truly I must,' she begged, squirming to get out of the black hole she'd dug herself into.

'I'm sure you can spell it out in very brief terms,' he bit out relentlessly.

Apologetic appeal was her last resort. 'I don't

think you want to know, James. I seem to have said too much already. Sorry...' She wriggled out of his grasp and grabbed her bag from her chair, hoping to make a fast exit.

'Dammit, Lucy! If Buffy has been maligning me behind my back...' He looked about to explode.

'No, no no! Not maligning you, James,' she emphatically assured him. 'Really, I'd call it flattering.'

'Meaning I didn't live up to it in your view?' he thundered.

Lucy lost it.

The words just came tumbling out in a frantic effort to put this disaster behind her.

'Buffy said you could go on and on. But since this was just a starter for the day, I quite understand that's all you wanted. We are supposed to be working, so it's only right to stop and get on with what we're really here for,' she reasoned, frenziedly trying to save the pride she had so successfully wounded, ruining everything in the process.

'A starter for the day?' he bellowed at her.

She almost jumped out of her skin. 'That's what you said!' she hurled back at him—the wound to her own pride. Then to mitigate all the offence, she blabbed, 'I'm sure you're a great lover when you don't have to think about work.'

'But you thought... *that was it?*'

He was in a towering fury.

To Lucy's shattered mind, escape was the only answer. 'I'll go and get ready for work,' she mumbled, heading for the door into the corridor, intending to bury herself in the washroom at the end of it.

'Hold it right there!' A blistering command.

She paused and cast him a look of desperate appeal. 'I do need to go.'

His eyes were flashing blue murder. 'All right!' he tersely conceded. 'But don't think we've finished this.'

Lucy trembled all the way down the corridor.

The realisation that she'd left James thinking she'd been merely trying out his equipment for size and stamina was deeply mortifying. She wasn't like that. She'd never been like that. In wanting Buffy out of his life, she'd done herself a damage that might very well be irretrievable.

And spoilt all the intense, amazing, ecstatic pleasure she had felt with James. An anguished moan ripped through her whole body as she closed and locked the washroom door. She rested her head against it, wishing she could die. No, wishing she had died before he had spoken *his* spoiling words. He'd given her a taste of heaven, and now she had completely blighted any chance of ever recapturing it.

Hell couldn't be worse than this, she thought in wretched despair. How was she going to face James again? How? She'd wanted so much to be special to him—uniquely special. She didn't want to live the rest of her life on her own and her heart said James Hancock was the one who could fill the lonely gaps better than anyone else ever would. But now…he probably wouldn't even want her as his secretary.

Unfortunately, she couldn't skulk in the washroom forever. *Don't think we've finished this,* he'd said. If she didn't reappear soon he might come and bang on the door. More shame!

Lucy forced herself to set about using the facilities. She felt like weeping buckets. Only the fear of losing her new contact lenses, which might swim out of her eyes on a flood of tears, held her inner misery contained. All the trouble she'd gone to in order to spark his interest and hold it…and she'd blown it all with her a self-defeating burst of pride, compounded by a bitter edge of black jealousy.

So what if he thought their intimacy had provided a great start to the day?

It was a start, wasn't it? A start she might have turned into more and more.

Why did she have to go and bring Buffy Tanner into it?

She stared at her kiss-swollen lips in the mirror above the sink, remembering the wild passion that had erupted between her and James. Mutual. Very, very mutual.

Don't think we've finished this!

Maybe there was still a chance, a feeble hope whispered. If she could straighten out the misunderstanding with James, confess her real feelings…her mind instantly shied from laying herself on such a vulnerable line. Best to assess his attitude first before diving headlong into more disaster. Which meant facing him.

Lucy took several deep, calming breaths. She brushed her hair until her hand was steady enough to re-apply lipstick without wobbling. Courage, she sternly told herself, deciding her appearance was as good as it was going to get, and there was no point in lingering in the washroom any longer. Waiting might not improve James' temper.

The walk back down the corridor felt like a walk to the guillotine. Her heart was in a nervous flutter. Her pulse was drumming in her ears. Remembering the flash of blue murder in James' eyes, she almost wished she had a black hood over her head. At least then she wouldn't see him working up to chopping her out of his life.

As it turned out, he was not waiting in her office. He had left the scene of the crime. Maybe he had decided to forget it and was setting up for work, all primed to put her firmly back in her secretarial place. Lucy was riven with uncertainty as to what to do now—wait for him to call her or take the initiative of telling him she was back?

The connecting door between their offices was open, beckoning her forward. She forced her somewhat tremulous legs to cross this last daunting distance, the need to see James—to gauge where she stood with him—driving her on.

He was not sitting at his desk. He was standing by the huge picture window, his back turned to her, his attention apparently fixed on the view of Sydney

Harbour. His back looked very stiff, his shoulders squared, and his arms were not hanging loose. Folded across his chest, Lucy surmised, which instantly formed a forbidding picture.

Panic seized her.

She had gone too far, tossing Buffy's words at him.

Her wayward tongue felt so thick she couldn't speak. She swallowed hard, desperately working some moisture into her mouth. No point in panicking. Best to confront whatever was going on in his mind. Then she'd know the worst. Open the conversation with business. That was relatively safe.

'Did anything happen yesterday that I should know about?' she asked, trying her utmost to project an efficient secretary voice.

He swung slowly around, a frosty glare in laser blue eyes.

Lucy's stomach was instantly reduced to jelly. He'd had second thoughts about what he'd done with her—second, third, fourth and fifth thoughts! In fact, he hated being faced with a reminder of it. His gaze sliced down and up her as though he wished he could disembowel her on the spot.

'We'll deal with this morning's e-mails first,' he stated icily.

'Oh! I thought since you arrived earlier than I did, you might have already dealt with them,' she gabbled, sick with relief that he was prepared to continue working with her.

'No, I haven't.' A positively arctic response.

'Fine. Okay. I'll get right onto them.'

She fled, her heart almost bursting with pain. It *was* finished...

James watched her swift exit, seething over her air of crisp efficiency. The saucy little skirt twitched provocatively as she turned her back on him, reminding him of how little she wore under it. How he was going to block that knowledge out of his mind for the rest of the day he didn't know, but be damned if he'd let her pull his strings any way she liked.

Whether Buffy had said those things or not, Lucy had definitely used them to gain the upper hand on him, reducing him to nothing more than an experience she'd fancied trying. He'd almost been goaded into whipping her off home with him for a day-long session in bed. But he didn't have to prove anything to her and he wasn't about to invite any further critical appraisal, either on his physique *or* his performance.

Lucy Worthington was not going to dominate him, not physically or mentally. She could play those manipulative games with her other lovers, but she'd find him a harder nut to crack. He'd satisfy her curiosity in his own good time, and on his terms. And one thing he was determined on with her— exclusive rights! If she thought she could juggle both him and Josh Rogan and anyone else she took a fancy to...

A bolt of shock hit him.

He strode to the connecting door, needing the question instantly settled. Lucy was seated at her desk, fingers tapping away at the keyboard with the firepower of a woodpecker—efficiency plus!

'Do you have a clean bill of health?' he shot at her.

Her head snapped towards him but her expression seemed totally blank, as though her mind hadn't connected to what he said.

'We just had unprotected sex, Lucy,' he bit out tersely. 'Is there a problem I should know about?'

'Oh!' Heat scorched her cheeks. 'Do you mean...could I get pregnant?'

'No.' He frowned over her interpretation. 'I mean you've been with Josh Rogan and God knows who else.'

Enlightenment dawned, along with a look of stricken horror. 'You've been with Buffy Tanner and God knows who else,' she shot back at him.

'I'm clean. I always use protection.'

'So do I. You have nothing to worry about.'

Clearly she was highly discomforted by the conversation. Her face was glowing with heat and her gaze jerked back to the monitor screen, her long loose hair swinging forward to block him out.

'Do I take it today was exceptional?' he drawled, pleased at getting under *her* skin and making her burn.

'You...umh...took me by surprise,' she excused in an embarrassed mumble.

'That doesn't usually happen to you?'

She visibly took a deep breath and looked him straight in the eye. 'No, it doesn't. What excuse do you have for not practising safe sex?'

'I was taken by surprise, too,' he answered, barely repressing a grin. 'Interesting, don't you think?'

'What do you mean?'

'Oh, just interesting,' he drawled and retreated to his office, his heart considerably lighter.

She hadn't gone along with him out of curiosity. There'd been no control at all, just hot wild passion all the way. Same as himself. Highly mutual desire running rampant.

It made James feel really good. He had the truth of it now. Measuring him and his performance had absolutely nothing to do with Lucy's response to him. Sheer wool over his eyes to put herself on top after the event. Well, it wasn't going to work. He'd have Lucy Worthington and he'd whittle down her defences until she confessed she wanted him every bit as much as he wanted her.

Let her simmer over what they had already shared. He was confident in his own mind she would want to try it again. It was only a matter of time. Meanwhile, he would revel in being master of the situation. Nothing to worry about.

James was in top humour for the rest of the day, getting through a prodigious amount of work with Lucy. He found it intensely gratifying that she was slightly on edge, watching him apprehensively as though on guard against being grabbed again and responding as she had this morning. It was further confirmation that this was new ground for Lucy Worthington. He'd stirred something in her that no other man had.

James exulted over this thought. He was also incredibly excited by it. In fact, he couldn't recall ever having been so excited by a woman. He could barely contain himself. He started watching the clock, determined on waiting out the full work-day, but impatient to set up another intimate encounter with his secretary.

He noticed Lucy checking her watch, too, as the afternoon drew closer to leaving time. Was she eager to get away? Finding the undeniable sexual tension between them tearing at her nerves? Control not so easy any more?

At ten to five she picked up a bunch of files from his desk to return them to the cabinet in her office. She walked so fast, the butterflies on her skirt flipped from side to side. Flight in progress, James thought, and was instantly compelled to lay down a trip-wire.

'Do you have any special plans for when we finish up here?' he tossed at her, keeping his tone casual.

She halted, her back going ram-rod straight. For several nerve-tingling seconds she stayed like that, not moving, not answering. James sensed an inner conflict raging, and with all his energy, willed her to give in to what *he* wanted. What he was convinced they both wanted.

'Nothing special,' she finally replied, half-turning

to look at him, her expression very guarded and wary. 'Why do you ask?'

He shrugged, leaned back in his chair, offered an encouraging smile. 'I wondered if you'd have dinner with me.'

'Dinner?' she repeated as though stunned by the idea.

'I'm not doing anything. If you're not doing anything...why not enjoy a meal together?' he reasoned affably.

She stared at him.

He could almost see the wheels going around in her head. He didn't really mean...just dinner. He meant bed and breakfast, too. And where would that lead? She had her job to consider. The sensible thing to do was...

'All right,' she said.

His heart leapt at the victory.

Temptation had won out.

'Good!' James approved, doing his utmost not to reveal his elation. He didn't want her to feel threatened in any way. He wanted her *with* him.

'Where were you thinking of going?' she asked.

'Where would you like?'

'I'm easy,' she said, and blushed a bright red.

'My place then,' he pressed decisively.

Her chin jerked up.

James suffered a searing stab of doubt. Had his eagerness pushed him too far too fast?

'Your place,' she repeated, her eyes glittering a

fierce challenge over the heat in her cheeks. 'In that case, I'll follow you there in my car.'

And leave whenever she wanted to.

James received the message loud and clear but he wasn't troubled by it. 'Fine,' he said, glancing at his watch. 'We'll take off in fifteen minutes or so. Okay?'

'Okay,' she agreed and made a fast exit from his office.

Done, James thought.

Although it wasn't a done deed yet, he reminded himself.

It was only the first step towards doing.

No...*undoing!*

And he grinned.

CHAPTER NINE

His place!

The intimacy of the invitation had Lucy's nerves in a riot. It felt as though the butterflies on her skirt had come alive and flocked into her stomach. If James had touched her as she accompanied him into the elevator which took them from their office floor to the basement car-park, she probably would have jerked away from him, frightened more of her own wild feelings than of him.

She stepped briskly to the rear of the compartment, leaving him to press the panel button and giving herself some space to get her mind clear and her skittish body under control. She'd wanted to step into his private life. This was her chance. Going to his place might not be very sensible, but what did she have to lose at this point?

Nothing.

Absolutely nothing.

And she had everything to gain.

Even if James had a sexual marathon in mind...so what? Hadn't she fantasised this kind of experience with him? She had to exude confidence, not apprehension. Seize the day. Seize the night. Seize anything he offered. There was no going back to the old worthy Miss Worthington image. Not after the raging heat of this morning's encounter on her office desk.

Besides, if for some reason, she decided this wasn't what she wanted, she had her own car to leave in whenever she chose. James surely understood that. The important factors were he was no longer angry with her and she had another chance with him.

'I don't know how to get to *your place*,' she said, doing her utmost to project a calm acceptance of this progression in their relationship. 'I know you live in Balmain, but...'

Balmain—one of the oldest suburbs of Sydney, like Woolloomooloo, where the dockyard workers had lived in earlier times. Now it was a very up-market trendy area, close to the inner city, the old terrace houses expensively renovated, trees cultivated along the narrow sidewalks, lots of fashionable eateries and the kind of shops that invariably catered to money.

'Just follow me in your car,' he advised. 'It's easier than explaining.'

'What if the traffic separates us?'

He smiled. 'I'll take very great care not to lose you, Lucy.'

It was like a warm caress all over her skin—that smile, that look in his eyes. He still wanted her. He was not going to lose her. And Lucy's fevered mind clutched his words, nursing them as though they were a promise of more than just sex between them—a promise of continuity, of value that went beyond a fleeting physical thing.

She definitely had to go with him. Her future was hanging on this journey. When the elevator stopped and the doors opened to the basement car-park, Lucy's legs moved automatically, compelled forward by a sense of commitment that had been seeded the moment she had decided to keep the red Alpha Spider convertible. Not the safe, sensible road. She was risking everything—*everything*—to have this man.

She took the car-keys out of her bag and pressed the unlocking device attached to them. James strode past her and opened the driver's door, a courtesy she hadn't expected. She paused, her heart drumming in her ears as her eyes searched his face for some sign of deeper feelings than desire.

'This isn't business, Lucy,' he stated pointedly, interpreting her pause as some feminist stance. 'You're my guest.'

He was treating her like a woman in his personal life, someone to be looked after, cared for. However facile the gesture was, it made Lucy feel like a winner already. 'Thank you,' she purred at him and slid into the driver's seat with as much feminine grace as she could manage.

He closed her into the car, his eyes gleaming satisfaction in her acquiescence. 'Sit on my tail,' he instructed, then grinned a devil-may-care challenge at her. 'Be aggressive if anyone tries to cut in.'

She watched him swing away to his black

Porsche—this man she had craved so long—and felt a fierce surge of possessive aggression. Let any woman try to cut in now that James had chosen to take up with her, and there'd be blood on the floor, including his if he proved fickle.

The drive to Balmain was something of a blur. With almost obsessive tunnel vision she saw only the black Porsche ahead of her, responding instinctively to its every move, slowing, stopping, accelerating, turning, feeling herself being irrevocably towed towards a place where her fate would be decided.

Was he taking her to a bachelor love-nest?

How many women had been there before her?

Would she become just one of a passing parade?

Stop it, she berated herself. What good was there in letting the past blight the present? James wanted *her* now. Nothing else mattered. She took a deep breath and muttered, 'Just take one step at a time. Live for the moment and meet the future as it comes, Lucy Worthington.'

She tried to focus more on where they were going since she would eventually have to find her way home. As they turned down a hill out of the main stream of traffic, she caught a glimpse of the harbour. The street was narrow with housing on both sides, most of the residences being terraces or semi-detached cottages, no obvious blocks of apartments. They travelled right to the end of the road before the black Porsche led her down a steep concrete driveway to a private parking area at the back of what had to be quite a large waterfront home.

Lucy was surprised. All the single career people she knew had minimum upkeep apartments, relatively free of maintenance problems which might take up their leisure time. A house such as this seemed too much to handle for a bachelor involved in a demanding business, as well as a high-flying social life. Nevertheless, it certainly reflected the kind of financial status that impressed people and undoubtedly made him even more attractive to those who counted such things.

Could she really compete with the likes of Buffy Tanner and all the socialites on the party circuit?

I'm here. They're not, Lucy firmly told herself, feasting her eyes on James as he skirted her car to open the driver's door. He wasn't as dashingly handsome as Josh, but he had a male animal magnetism that curled her toes. She wanted to see him stripped of clothes, wanted to feel the whole naked power of his masculinity. Everything had exploded on her this morning, all so sudden, so fast, but tonight...

The desire coursing through her was so strong, the touch of his hand was electric as he helped her out of the car, and her legs were definitely tremulous.

'Here we are, safely arrived,' James cheerfully remarked, guiding her to a flight of steps at the side of the house.

Probably the only *safe* thing done today, Lucy thought. 'You were right,' she acknowledged with a smile. 'I doubt I would have found this place by myself. Better to be led.'

'So now you can relax.'

Easier said than done. Lucy was wound up so tight, it was difficult to pluck out any line of normal conversation. 'Nice position you have here, right on the water,' she commented, sounding like a real estate person, buying or selling property.

'Yes. It's always good to come home to,' he replied, warm pleasure in his voice.

Was it especially good, having her with him, Lucy wondered—hoped—and would being in his home reveal more of the heart of the man?

There were three flights of steps down to the waterfront with landings marking the split levels of the house. The door James unlocked for her was off the first landing. Lucy preceded him into a hallway, her shoes clacking noisily on polished wooden floorboards, giving the house an empty sound. It made her very conscious of being really alone with him, and the door closing behind her punctuated the risk she was taking.

Every nerve in her body tensed but there was no sudden pouncing. James simply ushered her around a corner into a spacious foyer at the rear of a huge living area. As they stepped past the staircase which led upstairs, the whole ground floor, with all its dramatic interest, captivated her attention.

The foyer led into a kind of mezzanine level which virtually staged a magnificent black grand piano, and beyond it three exotically patterned sofas were grouped around a fire-place situated on the far wall which stretched up both storeys of the house to a domed ceiling of glass which flooded the area with light.

On the right of this level, a few steps led down to a dining-room, at the end of which were glass doors which gave a superb view of Sydney Harbour. On the left, matching steps led to an open-plan kitchen, its glass doors leading out to a large covered verandah which held more casual furniture for lounging or eating outside. Upstairs, a balcony ran around what had to be bedroom wings on either side of the mezzanine level with the high spectacular ceiling.

So struck was Lucy by all these fascinating features, she was barely aware of James moving past her to the kitchen, discarding his suitcoat and tie on a coat-rack along the way. This architectural wonder of a house, not to mention its prime location on the waterfront, had to be high in the millionaire class, and she felt swamped by what she had stepped into.

Would James ever see her as *belonging* in such a place as this? The office seemed like a world away. Yet he had chosen to bring her here, Lucy reminded herself.

'What would you like to drink?' he asked, jolting her back to the highly questionable issue of *why* he had invited her into the privacy of his home.

He had undone the top buttons of his shirt and was rolling up his sleeves. His virile energy hit Lucy anew, sending quivers through her stomach.

'Gin and tonic if you have it,' she answered, smiling ironically as she remembered having started all this recklessness last Friday night with a gin cocktail. *Mother's Ruin,* Josh had called it, and it would probably be her ruin, too, but she'd gone too far now to reconsider the wisdom of an intimate involvement with James Hancock.

'No problem,' he responded with an ironic smile of his own. 'You can hang up your bag on the coatrack.'

Getting rid of extraneous items.

Lucy took a deep breath to calm her nerves and did as he said. 'This must be a great place for entertaining guests,' she remarked, trying to sound natural.

'Yes. Most people find it friendly.'

He was busy making their drinks…ice-blocks and tonic water from a big, double-sided refrigerator, a lemon from a well-stocked bowl of fresh fruit, a bottle of Tanqueray gin from a liquor cupboard. Lucy stepped down to the kitchen level, ready to take her glass when it was ready. There was an island work-bench with stools around it and she was about to draw out a stool and sit on it when a voice rang out, freezing all activity.

'Darling! So glad you're home early…'

A female voice, rich with seductive delight, and coming from the balcony above them, the balcony that clearly led to bedrooms!

Lucy's stunned heart burst into a killer drum-beat. She shot a sizzling glare at James. 'Overlooked something?' she hissed, venomous words spilling forth. 'Like not telling *darling* up there that you play musical beds and her time was up?'

'She shouldn't be here,' he muttered, frowning up at the apparition on the balcony.

Lucy spun around to get an eyeful of the competition. The woman was striding along the balcony towards the staircase, a gorgeous silk gown patterned with fiery dragons billowing around her, tousled red hair being finger-raked back from a face which was still obscured from Lucy's view.

'I've been resting but it's definitely time for drinkies,' the woman declared, obviously expecting her wishes to be served.

Lucy burned. Let James sort this out in front of her. If he didn't send the woman packing, she would flay him alive with her tongue, not to mention telling his erstwhile lover what he'd been up to today. It was totally outrageous that he'd left this redhead in his bed, then within minutes of Lucy entering his office, slaking his sexual needs all over again with her. Buffy was certainly right about one thing. He was a pistol with women. And as far as Lucy was concerned, this was the showdown at the OK Corral.

'Why aren't you in Melbourne?' James suddenly thundered up at the scantily clad woman who was ruining his set scene.

So the bird was supposed to have flown, Lucy thought caustically.

'The black plague hit,' came the insouciant reply.

'I decided to escape any possibility of infection by getting right away from everyone.'

'There's been no news of a black plague,' James argued, vexation pouring from him.

'Chicken pox,' came the airy correction, an arm waving away any protest from him as she went on. 'What could be worse, darling? Apart from getting deathly ill, I'd run the risk of having my face scarred. I told Wilbur he'd just have to write me out of the show until the danger was over. It was all his fault anyway for bringing the poxy child into the cast.'

An actress. Probably as voluptuously endowed as Buffy Tanner, and just as fixated on the physical. Models, actresses… Lucy seethed over James' choice of women.

'You could have called me,' he shouted.

'What for? Wilbur understood. I'm not breaking the contract, just having a break. I haven't made any trouble for you.'

James muttered something violent under his breath and shot an anguished look at Lucy. She gave him back a merciless stare. Trouble was certainly coming if he didn't get rid of this woman. In fact, his ammunition would be highly endangered by a sharp knee to the groin if he didn't extract himself from the redhead in Lucy's favour.

'It's not what you think,' he grated.

'What is it then?' she asked sweetly.

'Pour me a gin and tonic, darling,' the order came from the top of the stairs.

'No wonder you've got the ingredients handy,' Lucy mocked.

'Make it a double gin,' the voice trilled. 'It's so good to be home.'

'Home? This is *her* home?' Lucy was so shocked her voice came out half-strangled.

'It's my mother,' James bit out, his face a study of intense frustration. 'And yes, this happens to be home to both of us.'

'Your mother...' Incredulity gripped Lucy, her mind automatically rejecting a situation that didn't seem at all real to her. 'You still live with your mother?'

'Something wrong with that?' he snapped.

It had to be real. The fierce blaze in his eyes clearly resented any implication that living with his mother was in any way odd at his age. So the woman coming down the stairs had to be Zoe Hancock, star of both stage and television, and currently a key-player in the high-rating hospital soap opera, *St Jude*.

Lucy had never met her in the flesh. She had seen her on screen and would definitely recognise her when they finally came face-to-face. She was also aware that this family background in show business gave James an edge in managing his clients, but she had no idea the mother-son relationship extended to sharing the same home.

'Well, it will be very interesting to meet her,' Lucy said decisively, and her eyes challenged him to make the introduction with good grace.

No way in the world was Lucy about to be treated as a piece of skirt he'd like to sweep under the mat. She might have been invited here for sex, but enjoying a family evening with James and Zoe Hancock suddenly loomed as an extremely attractive alternative...a fast-track insight into the very heart of their private lives.

CHAPTER TEN

JAMES gritted his teeth. Not only was the evening he'd planned ruined, but Lucy now had the impression he was living under his mother's thumb. Which meant she'd have to see for herself that he wasn't. Otherwise, any respect she held for him would be shot to pieces, and that was one outcome he wouldn't tolerate.

Whipping her away to dinner in a restaurant would not get him what he wanted. That was glaringly obvious. She was unsettled by the situation. There were questions to be answered, and if she wasn't satisfied, Lucy was perfectly capable of making unshakable judgements—mind over matter, regardless of how tempting the *matter* was.

'Oh, you have a guest! What an unexpected pleasure!' his mother trilled, sighting Lucy as she swanned down the stairs. A second thought clearly struck and she shot an arch look at James. 'Is this why you sounded a bit cross? Am I *de trop,* darling?'

'Not at all,' he dryly assured her, resigning himself to the inevitable. 'Lucy was just saying she'd be interested to meet you.'

'Lucy...' A warm, welcoming smile was beamed at her. 'Do please forgive the deshabille—' a graceful gesture excused the exotic dressing-gown '—but

113

I am at home, you understand.' She looked expectantly at James. 'Lucy who, darling? Don't leave me in the dark.'

'Lucy Worthington…Zoe Hancock.'

'Worthington… Worthington… I'm simply terrible with names. Should I know it?'

'Lucy is my secretary,' James stated to cut the agony short.

'*The* secretary?' His mother looked at Lucy in astonishment—looked her up and down—then raised her eyebrows at him as though he'd lied through his teeth.

'A double gin coming up,' he said, refusing to get into explanations about Lucy's change of image.

'Have you been my son's secretary very long, Lucy?' his mother pressed on with totally unabashed curiosity.

'About eight months,' came the matter-of-fact reply.

'Well, I must say James made you sound quite different to what you are.'

'On the contrary,' he cut in. 'I said my secretary was the most sensible woman I've ever met and she is still the most sensible woman I've ever met.'

He added a twist of lemon to the drinks and carried them to the two women, seizing the opportunity to clear up the situation since Lucy might well decide any further intimacy with him was unwise and she was better off out of it.

'What I didn't tell you and what I've come to realise,' he said to his mother, then turned his gaze to Lucy, deliberately locking eyes with her, 'is that she is also the sexiest woman I've ever met.'

He could feel the power drill of Lucy's brain boring into his. *'Ever?'*

She was smart, utterly delectable, and infinitely exciting in her ability to challenge. 'Ever,' he confirmed emphatically.

Electricity crackled from her. 'Surpassing the beautiful Buffy?'

'Buffy is no longer even desirable.' It was the absolute truth.

'You seem rather fickle in your desires.'

'Superficial distractions. I've had one constant desire burning in me for some time now. Only on Friday night did I discover it was mutual.' She couldn't deny that and James topped it with more undeniable truth. 'As with everything you do, Lucy, you hid your light under a bushel with superb efficiency.'

She blushed. Something she couldn't control, James noticed, which excited him even further, wondering if her whole body blushed. At the very least, it was a sign of vulnerability to him, and nothing was going to stop him from exploiting that vulnerability.

His mother coughed. 'This conversation...'

'Is necessary.' He flicked her a derisive look. 'When you floated out on the balcony, Lucy thought I was playing musical beds.'

'Me?' She laughed, reached out and patted Lucy's

arm indulgently. 'My dear! What a compliment, taking me for one of James' women.'

'He does tend to run through them rather quickly,' came the acerbic comment.

'Perhaps because they fawn on him,' his mother remarked with knowing amusement. 'I can see you don't. Very sensible.'

'Well, I guess you have the best standpoint to judge these things, Mrs Hancock,' She shot him a look that was loaded with dubious thoughts as she added, 'having lived with James so long.'

He tensed, realising he hadn't won anything yet. Lucy's guard remained up and this moving straight into the question of his sharing a home with his mother was a clear signal her mind was still assessing the situation. Her hand-bag was in easy stepping distance, hanging on the coat-rack, and although he'd put a glass in her hand, that could be quickly disposed of.

'Shall we take our drinks out to the verandah?' he swiftly suggested, wanting to put distance between her and her car-keys.

'Good idea! Fresh air to blow thoughts of the plague away,' his mother approved, collecting Lucy as she moved forward. 'And please call me Zoe, dear. Hancock is actually my maiden name. I didn't marry James' father, you know.'

James winced at his mother's garrulous habit of letting everyone know he was a bastard. Supposedly it reflected well on her for shouldering the task of bringing him up alone—the brave single mother—

but it always made him feel belittled, having been fathered by a man who hadn't cared enough to stick around.

'I'm sorry. I didn't know,' Lucy muttered, sounding embarrassed by the revelation.

'It simply wouldn't have worked,' his mother burbled on. 'A brief fire in our lives, not a lasting passion. I didn't marry at all until I met my wonderful Hugh, and James was fifteen by then.'

She was off and running and, James knew from experience, impossible to stop with a new audience to lap up the more colourful details of their lives.

'Should I know your Hugh?' Lucy asked, being drawn in by the excessive story-telling.

'Really, James,' his mother huffed. 'Haven't you told Lucy anything about your life?'

'I'm sure you'll make up the deficit,' he replied, ushering them out to the verandah. At least his mother was adept at carrying guests with her, which was something to be grateful for. He was acutely aware of how elusive Lucy could be.

'Hugh…Hugh Greenaway…was a marvellous father to James,' his mother rattled on. 'Just what he needed after years of being dragged around with a bunch of actors, living in temporary digs and having to fit in with the mad hours we worked. It's amazing he wasn't taken away by social workers, now that I think about it.'

'I had lots of aunties and uncles, remember?' James put in dryly, trying to correct any impression of being an object of pity.

He wouldn't swap his childhood for any other. As an education in life and people, it had covered a very broad spectrum. Yet there had been many times he'd envied other boys their fathers and the activities they shared with them. If he'd had a father like Hugh, right from the beginning…

'But it was a rackety existence, darling,' his mother insisted. 'Always changing schools.'

That wasn't good, James silently agreed, but he'd learnt to go with the flow.

'Sit here, Lucy.'

She waved to the cane armchair adjacent to the fan-backed one she always favoured herself—the queen taking her throne, usually surrounded by courtiers. There was only Lucy to entertain this evening, and James watched them sit down together, confident his mother would hold her audience captive for a while.

'I'll get some nibbles,' he said and back-tracked to the kitchen, relieved to have Lucy settled and within easy reaching distance.

She could make what she liked of what his mother told her. It was irrelevant to him…as long as she stayed.

Lucy's mind was in a whirl, knocked for a loop by the idea that James had fancied her for some time, even *before* the charity ball! Was it true? And was Buffy—every other woman—completely out of the picture now? Did he really think she was the sexiest female he'd ever met? It felt…too much to believe.

On top of that she was now sitting here with his mother, which was as unexpected as everything else, and she was being fed information so fast she could barely take it in. With James having taken himself back to the kitchen, relieving her of the distraction of his overpowering presence, she tried to recollect herself enough to focus on Zoe Hancock.

The older woman had glorious hair, thick with curls and waves, its rich colour undoubtedly provided by a hairdresser since she had to be in her fifties, but her pale skin suggested she had once been a natural redhead. Her face was relatively unlined, perhaps due to cosmetic surgery, yet it radiated a vivid personality through the fascinating mobility of her mouth and expressive blue eyes. James had the same eyes but Lucy could see no other similarity to his mother.

His father—the brief fire in Zoe Hancock's life—must have been in the tall, dark and handsome mould. Lucy wondered if he knew he'd fathered a son. How brief was *brief*? From what she'd been told so far, he'd played no part in James' upbringing. She wondered if James felt as deprived as she had by her father's desertion.

'This was Hugh's place. I think I fell in love with it before I fell in love with him,' Zoe remarked, gazing at the view down the harbour to the great coat-hanger bridge that spanned it. She heaved a sigh and flashed a wry smile at Lucy. 'He left it to us when he died, but I'm away more than I'm home these days. It's lucky James is always here to look after everything.'

'I imagine he feels lucky to have the pleasure of it.'

She nodded. 'It's the only real home he's ever known. God knows where he might have ended up without Hugh settling him into a proper education and guiding him through law.'

'Guiding him?' Lucy queried, thinking James was not the kind of person to be guided anywhere he didn't want to be led.

'My incredibly clever husband was a top-flight barrister,' Zoe proudly declared. 'He taught James all the tricky things about contracts, putting him wise on what to look out for in the entertainment business. That's a good part of why he's so successful at managing his clients.'

'Meticulous attention to detail,' Lucy agreed, privately reasoning that James had probably taken every opportunity to pick Hugh Greenaway's brains, already knowing where he wanted to go. He wasn't a follower. Having worked so closely with him, Lucy was fairly sure James always had and always would forge his own path.

'There is the personality angle, too,' she pointed out to his mother. 'He's very good with people.'

Zoe laughed. 'Well, something of me had to rub off on him.'

That could be so, but coping with all the honorary aunts and uncles and constant changes of school had more likely made getting along with people a sur-

vival art, Lucy thought. She wondered what, if anything, had ever touched him deeply. Maybe superficial relationships had become a habit—here today,
gone tomorrow, enjoying whatever pleasure they
gave him.

'Have you been a widow long?' she asked, really
wanting to know more of James' relationship with
his stepfather.

'Longer than I was a wife,' she answered ruefully.
'I only had nine years with Hugh. He loved sailing
and always crewed for a friend in the Sydney to
Hobart yacht race. Ten years ago a dreadful storm
blew up during one of those races and Hugh was
swept overboard, drowning before he could be res-
cued. It was a wicked, wicked waste of a life.'

'He died as he lived, doing what he wanted,'
James sliced in, carrying out a cheeseboard with a
plate of crackers and olives. 'And if he hadn't been
a risk-taker, you wouldn't have married him. One
thing he didn't do was waste his life, playing everything safe.'

His gaze swung to Lucy and the challenge in his
eyes thumped into her heart. It was what she had
resolved herself—not to play safe—and he wasn't
playing safe, either. They were both risking their
work relationship, compelled to explore a desire that
was by no means fulfilled...yet! Where it would
lead—where it would end—neither of them knew.
A brief fire or a lasting passion?

'You've told me that a thousand times, darling,

but it doesn't stop me missing him when I come home,' Zoe said plaintively.

James set the food down on a coffee-table within easy reach of the armchairs and shot his mother a sharply inquiring look. 'Have you broken up with Wilbur?'

'No, no. Wilbur's a dear sweet man and he understands me. We do share a lot, but...'

'There will never be another Hugh,' came the quiet admonition.

Zoe rolled her eyes at him. 'Do you have to be so sensible, James?'

'It's my job,' he returned dryly. 'Excuse me while I get my drink.'

'Honestly!' Zoe huffed at Lucy. 'He's been like that since he was a boy, making me face up to things instead of letting me float along in my usual haphazard fashion. Is he a terribly bossy boss?'

'I've always found him very reasonable,' Lucy replied, which was true, for the most part.

'Ah, yes, but you're sensible, too. Like minds, no doubt.'

Lucy had to smile. Being sensible was certainly not part of the current equation. But it was interesting to learn Zoe Hancock's view of her son. It seemed that she looked to him to keep her life in order and there was no such dependency the other way. No mother domination at all. James was, without a doubt, what he had made of himself, and Lucy found that strength of mind and purpose immensely attractive.

He re-emerged from the kitchen, jiggling his drink as he took command of the conversation. 'So, am I to understand there's no problem in Melbourne apart from the threat of chicken pox?' he demanded of his mother. 'You haven't come flying home for any other reason?'

'Truly, darling, everything's fine,' she assured him. 'Wilbur doesn't want me to risk my health, either. It's just a precaution, nothing more.'

'I'm glad to hear it.'

He settled onto the cane armchair directly across the table from where Lucy sat, leaned forward, cut off a slice of brie from the selection of cheeses, spread it on a cracker and offered it to her, his vivid blue eyes appealing for her to take it.

'Thank you,' she murmured, her pulse beginning to gallop as he watched her lift it to her mouth and bite into it.

A sensual smile played on his lips as he proceeded to serve both his mother and himself. Lucy remembered how sensational his mouth was...kissing hers...and as enlightening as Zoe Hancock's presence had been, she wished his mother elsewhere.

'It's such a lovely, balmy evening,' Zoe remarked. 'Who would have thought it would still be this warm in March?'

'A late summer,' James said and gave Lucy a look that simmered with hot invitation. 'Would you like to have a swim in the pool before dinner?'

Pool? She quickly recalled the flight of steps going down beyond the landing that must lead onto this verandah and realised there was a ground level she hadn't yet seen. 'I'd love to, but...' Surely he didn't expect her to go skinny-dipping with his mother here, though she squirmed sensually at the wicked thought of swimming naked with him. She'd never swum nude in her life, but with James...

'But what?' he pressed, offering her the dish of olives.

She shook the wild fantasy out of her head. 'I don't have a swimming costume with me,' she answered ruefully, choosing a black olive.

'We keep a selection for guests in the cabana. I'm sure there'll be something to fit you.'

'Oh!' She almost choked on the olive as his eyes burned into hers, feeding images of them being in the water together, none of them remotely connected to actually swimming. The *something to fit her*...did he mean him? She could barely catch enough breath to answer, 'Okay. Sounds great!'

She could feel the strength of mind and purpose she so admired encompassing her, tugging on her like an irresistible magnet, and every nerve in her body was dancing in response.

'What were you thinking of doing for dinner?' Zoe asked.

'Whatever appeals when we feel like it,' James answered, his eyes still locked on Lucy's, promising to please her in every way. 'There's plenty to choose from in the refrigerator.'

Could his mother feel the sexual energy being

emitted? Was he always so open about it in front of her? Even being conscious of his mother being a spectator, Lucy couldn't tear her eyes from his.

'Then why don't I prepare something while you two have your swim?' Zoe brightly suggested.

'Fine!' James agreed. 'Is there anything you particularly don't like—' He paused, raising goosebumps on Lucy's skin as he let the question linger suggestively before adding '—in the way of food, Lucy?'

She sucked in a deep breath, trying to focus on the practical question being asked. 'I don't really enjoy burn-your-mouth food like chillies and hot Indian curries.'

He smiled. 'No de-sensitising your taste-buds.'

For kissing, Lucy instantly thought, though she had never connected such things before this. It was James, messing with her mind, the desire emanating from him exciting her own madly wanton urges.

'Then that's settled,' Zoe said with satisfaction, apparently happy to accommodate her son's program for the evening. 'I'll just potter around the kitchen and see what inspires me.' She aimed a warmly encouraging smile at Lucy. 'It occurs to me that I've been rattling on about our life and I know nothing about yours, apart from being James' secretary. Do tell me more.'

This distraction was deeply unwelcome, yet courtesy demanded she answer something. Lucy took a quick sip of her gin and tonic to cool herself down. It was difficult to pluck anything sensible out of her fevered brain with James still watching her, listening intently, alert to her every response, both verbally and physically. Her whole consciousness was vibrating on a more immediate level—what was going to happen next, not what had made up her life before this.

'I really have nothing out of the ordinary to relate,' she said with a dismissive shrug. The last thing she wanted was to sound boring when James was finding her exciting...*the sexiest woman he'd ever met!* Somehow she had to live up to that, keep his interest running.

'Where do your family live?' Zoe persisted.

'At Gosford. But I don't really have a family. Only a mother.' Like him, she quickly reasoned. Common ground. It was okay to say that much. She wanted a bond between them that went beyond work and sexual excitement, and she exulted at the gleam of interest she saw in his eyes. 'I was an only child,' she added, eager to re-inforce the bond, let him know she'd been fatherless, too. 'My parents were divorced when I was very young and my father went off travelling. I have no idea where he is.'

'Your mother didn't re-marry?' Zoe asked, seeking more background.

'No. I guess you could say she became a career person, preferring to be on her own,' Lucy answered reluctantly.

'Ah!' James murmured, as though she'd just said something enlightening.

Lucy's skin prickled. What did he think she had just revealed?

'What does your mother do?' Zoe asked curiously.

'She runs a health food business,' Lucy answered, still wondering why the career tag was meaningful to James.

'With all the nutritional fads and diets these days, it must be a thriving business,' Zoe pressed.

'It suits my mother,' Lucy replied, not wanting to comment further. She couldn't guess what either James or his mother were reading into this information and she felt discomforted by Zoe's persistent probing for more background. Wasn't it enough that she was a person in her own right?

'Well, healthy food is fine, but all dietitions say it should be accompanied by exercise,' James drawled, pushing up from his chair and giving his mother a look that warned her off any further cross-examination. 'If you'll excuse us...'

'Of course, darlings.' She eloquently gestured her generosity of spirit over the move. 'Do go and enjoy the pool. Work up an appetite for dinner. I wouldn't want my culinary efforts wasted.'

Relieved to be off the hook where his mother was concerned, Lucy quickly put her glass down and eagerly took the hand James offered to pull her up from her chair. Just the feel of his fingers closing around hers set her body abuzz with appetites that had nothing to do with food.

'Take your time,' James advised his mother. 'We're not in any hurry for dinner, are we, Lucy?'

'No,' she agreed.

But there was a sense of urgency pulsing between them, and as James led her off the verandah to the steps that presumably took them to the pool and cabana, the hand holding hers tightened to a hotly possessive grip and her heart started drumming in her ears.

Her mind shut down on where this was leading.

James was orchestrating the moves.

Let him lead.

CHAPTER ELEVEN

'THE pool is solar-heated. The water is like warm silk this time of the evening,' James told her as they descended the flight of steps.

His voice was like warm silk, Lucy thought, a sensual encouragement to feel all there was to feel. She shivered in anticipation. 'Do you swim every day?' she asked, tinglingly aware of his strong, muscle-toned physique.

'Depends on the weather, but most days, yes.' He flashed her a wicked grin. 'I enjoy swimming and it's supposedly the best physical exercise. It makes keeping fit a pleasure.'

Lucy's mind instantly skipped to the other physical pleasures that undoubtedly gave his body a good work-out. If Buffy had spoken the truth...but she wasn't going to think about Buffy, or any of his other women. This was here and now with her.

They reached ground level and there was the pool stretching out in front of them, clear blue water rippling in the balmy breeze. Most of the area surrounding it was paved with slabs of blue-green slate, but along the high side fences of the property, ensuring privacy, was a profusion of fern-trees, palms and tropical shrubs with shiny, colourful leaves, creating an environment that was visually exotic as well as inviting total relaxation.

Underneath the shade of the verandah were sun-loungers and occasional tables. Behind them was a third level to the house, presumably what they called the cabana, a large glass-fronted room, its layout curtained from view. James released Lucy's hand, removed a key from under a pot-plant, unlocked a sliding glass door, opened it, lifted the curtain aside and waved Lucy into what appeared to be more a guest suite than a casual entertaining area.

Her gaze was instantly drawn to the queen-size bed, her imagination running riot with the sexual fantasies she'd woven around James in the long months of her employment as his secretary. Only vaguely did she hear the click of the door closing, the rustle of the curtain dropping back into place, but all her senses leapt into vibrant life as James' arms wound around her waist, scooping her back against him, and the warmth of his breath caressed her ear as he lowered his head to hers to murmur seductively intimate words.

'I've been anticipating this moment all day and I can't wait any longer. Say it's what you came for...that you can't bear not to feel again what exploded between us this morning.'

His hands moved up under her top, taking possession of her breasts, kneading them, revelling in their soft giving to his touch. Her bottom was nestled against his groin and there was no doubting the urgency of his desire, his arousal only too evident in its hard, erotic pressure. Lucy was dazed, thrilled that he could want her so much, that this morning's passion had not abated and was just as strong—stronger—now.

'Say it, Lucy. Take the risk. Break your rules. Don't hide from me any more. You can't anyway. I know.'

His voice throbbed with confident knowledge.

She didn't care that he knew what she felt.

She didn't care about anything but having him.

'Yes...' The admission poured from her heart. 'I do want more of you.'

More than he was thinking of, but it would come, Lucy told herself. It had to, or this flood of feeling for him was a terrible misdirection of nature.

'Yes,' he echoed, a hiss of triumphant satisfaction. 'So let it *be* more. No clothes this time.'

His hands moved swiftly, whipping off her top. Momentarily freed of his embrace, Lucy whirled around to face him, her eyes blazing with her own need to have him stripped, as well. 'You, too, James. This is a two-way deal,' she insisted feverishly, her fingers attacking the buttons of his shirt, uncaring if he thought her brazen. It wasn't right, James taking without giving her all of himself. The word, *mutual,* was pounding through her mind.

He laughed, seemingly elated by her positive counter-action, pulling off his shirt as she opened it. His tanned skin was gleamingly taut over his chest and arm muscles, somehow glorifying his beautiful masculinity which was so sleek and strong, everything female in Lucy started fluttering in a purely pagan response to the man he was. Even the nest of black hair across his chest suggested an animal virility that touched something deeply primitive in her.

Impossible to stop her fingers speading through that hair, luxuriating in the feel of it. Under her palm the thump of his heart transmitted a charge to her own heart, an exultant pulse of joy and need that she knew, beyond any possible doubt, was intensely mutual—such exhilarating, intoxicating knowledge, like swimming in dreams that had taken on flesh and blood reality.

'Stopping there, Lucy?' James teased, his voice husky now, affected by her absorption in him.

She looked up into eyes that had darkened to deep blue. 'You had the advantage of me this morning,' she reminded him. 'I didn't get to touch you.'

'Satisfy yourself then. As I will.'

He reached around her waist, unclipping and unzipping her skirt. Driven to match him, she slid her own hands down over his stomach to unfasten his trousers, wanting him stripped at the same time, both of them equally naked. Clothes were discarded in a rush of eagerness, shoes, too, everything tossed aside with a wild sense of abandoning all inhibitions because this reality was a thousand times more exciting than anything she could dream.

At last she was free to know all of him and he crushed her to him as though the need to imprint her flesh and blood reality on his was of the utmost urgency, as though he, too, had wanted it for months and the waiting and fantasising were finally over.

'No pins—' he growled, grabbing a fistful of hair, winding it around his fingers '—and all buttons undone.'

'I didn't have buttons,' she said distractedly, revelling in the lean line of his hips, the powerful hardness of his thighs, the taut curve of his buttocks, filling her hands with every tactile sensation within her reach, even as she soaked in the sheer bliss of feeling her breasts squashed against the heat of his bare chest and his erection furrowing her stomach. He was perfect—incredibly, wonderfully perfect.

'You've been primly pinned and buttoned up from the day I employed you, Lucy Worthington,' he gruffly accused. 'But I've got you now—the woman I always sensed was underneath it all.'

Always?

He started walking her backwards, dominantly purposeful. Lucy found the movement so exciting, her mind barely grasped the idea that James had been thinking of her as a woman, not just as his worthy secretary.

'Why did you never say anything?' she cried, remembering the anguish of her own secret wanting which he'd given no hint of returning.

He tumbled her onto the bed, kneeling over her, hauling her into a more comfortable position, smiling into her eyes. 'I liked the tantalising mystery...the way you fenced with me.' He lifted her arms up over her head, holding her wrists to keep them there. 'But more and more I've wanted you like this, Lucy, open to me, wanting me, responding with the passion I sensed in you.'

Was it true? Had the attraction been there all along, building towards this on both sides?

He bent and ran his tongue between her lips, making them tingle. She lifted a leg and caressed the back of his knee with her foot, instinctively denying him complete mastery over her. His head jerked up. Then with a rumbling growl he released her wrists, burrowing an arm under her hips as he plundered her mouth with a swift challenging drive to arouse and excite the passion he wanted to feast on.

Lucy gave it to him, as greedy as he was for the same ravishing intimacy, the same heady explosion of sensation, the same sense of an ecstatic inner sharing that broke all normal boundaries, that zoomed them into a world owned only by them.

She felt the hot hardness of his penis being moved against the soft moistness at the apex of her thighs, caressing, inciting an almost unbearable excitement, back and forth, back and forth until she wrenched her mouth from his and cried for its insertion. 'Enough! I need you now...now....'

And he plunged into her, so deliciously full and fast, dispelling the terrible yearning for him, answering the throbbing need with a force that arched her body in exquisite satisfaction, and she could feel her inner muscles convulsing with the intense pleasure of it, squeezing him, relaxing to let him pump the sheer splendour of this fantastic togetherness higher and higher, climbing to peak after peak of quivering ecstasy, her legs wrapped around him, driving him on, her hands blindly urging, her eyes closed, her whole being inwardly focused on this wildly compelling mating with James...James...her man...and she his woman...bonding...melding...

Climax!

Shattering in its power, tempestuous in its rolling rush through every cell in her body, blissful in its aftermath.

Then a long, sweet, sensual kiss, gentling hands, contented sighs, a slow, reluctant parting.

They looked at each other, in their eyes a wordless acceptance of having experienced something special. How special it was to him, Lucy had no idea. In her need to draw some heart-warming admission from him, she remembered a claim he had made earlier today.

'You said you always used protection,' she blurted out, secretly—anxiously—watching for some sign that it was different with her for a host of reasons that were emotional, as well as physical.

His mouth curved with some private pleasure. 'I didn't want anything to come between us.'

'But to break a personal rule...'

He smiled into her eyes. 'Isn't that what we're both doing, Lucy? Breaking all the rules we set ourselves? Messing with our work relationship because we wanted this?'

The realisation that it wasn't sensible for him, either, gave her hopes a boost. But giving in to temptation after eight months...was that really a sign that she was special to him or merely an admission that desire had finally overridden good business sense?

'Besides, you said I didn't need protection and you wouldn't lie about that, Lucy,' he went on. 'Not about control. It's too important to you.' He trailed his fingers down over her stomach making her flesh leap at his touch. 'Even just now you called the shots.'

'Hardly,' she protested, amazed that he thought she had any control at all over what she felt.

His eyes teased. 'Didn't I move to your command?'

Her mind jolted with the memory of Josh inadvertently suggesting he was a slave to her whims and James then thinking she had dominatrix tendencies. But surely he didn't really believe that.

'I don't remember standing over you with a whip. More like you did what *you* wanted, as well,' she replied, mocking his assertion.

He laughed, a happy gloating in his eyes. 'No complaint. But I shall contest your timing in the next round.'

'Round? Is that what you call it?' Again her heart fluttered apprehensively. Did he see this as some kind of contest he had to win? Was that what had *really* excited him?

'There's always a battle of the sexes,' he answered sardonically, stroking her hair away from her face. 'And I see no surrender in your eyes. In all probability you're plotting the next move.'

She didn't want a battle with him. Never had. Just two people finding love and holding onto it. Why did it have to be so complicated between them? Couldn't he simply feel they were right for each other?

She shouldn't have deceived him with Josh. Yet hadn't that deception triggered the change in his attitude towards her, heightening his interest and sharpening the desire he'd repressed for the sake of not messing with his business set-up?

Desperately needing time to think, she said, 'If we don't soon move to the swimming pool your mother will start to wonder.'

'Ah! To the shower!'

He swung off the bed, scooped her up and carried her to an ensuite bathroom. Caveman style he hoisted her over his shoulder as he opened the door to the shower stall and turned on the taps. Lucy didn't get any time to think. He no sooner set her on her feet under a streaming spray of water than he grabbed a bar of soap and started sliding it over her.

Her hair was getting wet and it would be a mess— was the last rational thought she had. He soaped her breasts with a slow sensuality that trapped her into a fascinated thrall. It was as though he was rapt in the structure of them, and as fascinated as she was by their response to his caressing. Then the glide of the soap over her abdomen and down between her legs. Never had she been washed so intimately, and she felt his fingers circling, drawing more intense excitement.

Mindlessly, she lifted her hands to his shoulders, instinctively seeking a steadying support. The hair on his chest was plastered into tight curls. His naked body somehow seemed magnified this close— big...big all over, overwhelmingly male, intensely physical, powerfully sexual.

Suddenly he lifted her, lifted her against the shower wall and his mouth was lashing her breasts, licking, sucking, wildly tugging on her tightly extended nipples, and she was embracing his head with a fierce desire to hold him there, her legs encircling him just as possessively, and when he pushed inside her again, her only thought was a sweetly savage... Oh yes! Yes...yes...her whole being exulting in the compulsive madness of it, the incredible arc of pleasure from her breasts to her womb, the pumping of it to another intense climax. She was totally consumed by the tumultous power of it, even when it was over.

James gently eased her down to stand on her own two feet. 'This could get addictive,' he murmured, his eyes simmering with a lust for more. 'But I guess we'd better go and swim.'

'Yes,' she managed to reply, struggling to appear as composed as he seemed about what they'd just shared.

He turned off the taps, stepped out of the stall, grabbed a towel and wrapped it around her, touching her cheek in an oddly tender salute as he said, 'I'll find you something to wear.'

Had he given up the idea of *battle,* she wondered, watching him leave the ensuite bathroom, aware of every nerve-ending in her body buzzing with pleasure and wantonly anticipating being served with more and more of it. No control at all, she dazedly thought, and decided it didn't matter. She could only hope that whatever was driving James would last beyond tonight because she was beyond controlling anything.

He came back with a silvery maillot. 'This should fit. Stretchy fabric.'

There was no bra structure in it and the leg-line was cut high to her hips. The thin nylon provided little more than a second skin over what it covered. Didn't matter, she reasoned again. Only he was going to see her. Possibly his mother, too, she belatedly remembered, but that would only be in the pool if Zoe Hancock happened to look over the verandah railing.

The brief black costume James had put on was just as revealing. Her gaze strayed to the heavy bulge at the apex of his thighs. Three times today already, Lucy thought, wishfully—lustfully—wondering if he was planning on more. It was a terrible thing about lust. Having it so brilliantly satisfied seemed to generate more.

'Let's go,' he said, taking her hand.

Even that contact felt intensely sexual.

He released it when they reached the edge of the pool, letting her dive in alone.

The water *was* warm and silky, a lovely sensual liquid flow around her body, doing nothing at all to cool her mind, inciting an even deeper seduction towards simply luxuriating in feeling. Her hair which had been heavily wet from the shower, floated around her, weightless, as she turned on her back and floated.

'You look like a mermaid,' James said, treading water beside her.

She smiled, enjoying her own wicked thoughts as she replied, 'Having a tail might be inconvenient.'

He laughed, and his pleasure in her was a further intoxication. She started swimming, spurted on by a glorious burst of energy and wanting to share all his pleasures with him. He didn't attempt to make a competition of it, matching her leisurely stroke, apparently content with the companionship, which warmed Lucy's heart. When she tired and rested at one end of the pool, he stopped with her, reaching out to draw her into an embrace. She went willingly, loving the slow entanglement of his legs with hers.

His eyes were midnight-blue in the gathering twilight of the evening. They searched hers, as though wanting the response of her mind as well as her body. 'I'm beginning to think we're natural partners…at work and play,' he said quietly, seriously.

Yes, her heart sang. She smiled. 'We seem to fit together very well.'

His answering smile was loaded with sensual appreciation. 'In every sense. So I think we should explore how far it goes, don't you?'

'James... Lucy?' Zoe Hancock called from above. 'Are you coming up soon? I've got everything ready to start cooking when you give the word.'

His mother! And soon to come—facing her across a dinner table! Lucy's lifetime habit of looking respectable—according to her own mother—came crashing into prominence. 'I'll need at least twenty minutes to do something with my hair,' she warned James in an anxious whisper.

He frowned quizzically at her, as though the state of her hair was totally irrelevant to him, then called back, 'Give it half an hour and we'll be ready to eat.'

'Half an hour,' Zoe repeated. 'That's fine...' Her voice trailed away.

James frowned again at Lucy. 'Don't be worried by my mother. She has nothing to do with us.'

'She's here...' *Summing me up, assessing me, and she'll discuss me with you when I'm gone...* but Lucy choked up on admitting she wanted his mother's approval. It assumed too much of their relationship. 'We can't keep ignoring that, James,' she pleaded.

'Agreed,' he conceded. 'Just don't let her interfere with this.'

He kissed her with ravishing intensity, wiping out the rest of the world. He peeled the flimsy maillot from her body, baring it to his again, and the water lapping them made the flesh to flesh contact even more erotic. When he hauled her up to sit her on the edge of the pool, Lucy was still rocking from the explosion of sensation spiralling through her. The maillot was drawn off and tossed onto the paving behind her. He moved between her legs, opening them wide.

'Lean back, Lucy, and think of me wanting to do this, and more, as you sit at the dinner-table with my mother.' He grinned wickedly. 'And know I'll be thinking of it, too.'

He parted the intimate folds of her sex and kissed her there, with even more ravishing intensity than he had kissed her mouth. Lucy automatically arched back, her arms supporting her as waves of pleasure issued from the exquisite caressing. He hooked her legs over his shoulders and she felt his tongue delve inside her, swirling, inciting an incredible excitement, driving her into another shuddering release which he soothed with gentle stroking until the quivering ceased.

'Hold onto what you feel now,' he murmured, his eyes burning with hot purpose. 'Don't let it go no matter what my mother says or does.'

Impossible to let it go. The acute sexual awareness he had stirred was pulsing chaotically through her bloodstream, throbbing through her mind.

He left her alone while she showered and washed her hair, going to fetch her bag from upstairs so she could apply fresh make-up and use her own hairbrush as she wielded the hair-dryer in the bathroom. But she didn't feel parted from him. Not for a moment. It was as though he had infiltrated her entire being.

Every sense was heightened with this feeling when he came back. While she attended to her hair and face, he was in the bathroom with her, showering and towelling himself dry, and she could barely stop herself from staring at him, so entranced was she by the naked physique of the man.

Even when he dressed she kept seeing him as he was without clothes. He watched her, too, waiting for her to be ready to confront his mother again, and all the time she felt his sizzling desire for every possible intimacy with her.

To Lucy, dinner with his mother seemed to take place on two levels. One appeared to be relatively normal. Conversation was carried on and she took some part in it because she heard herself speaking from time to time. The meal Zoe Hancock had cooked—a beef and vegetable stir-fry with noodles—was eaten, although Lucy couldn't recall tasting any of it.

On a secret and far more dominant level was the unrelenting and explicit message in every look James gave her—a simmering promise of more and more of what she had already experienced with him. It made her breasts tingle. It shot little shivers down her thighs. Her inner muscles clenched with the memory of all he'd made her feel—was still making her feel.

She grew so self-conscious of her response to him that she felt his mother couldn't fail to sense what was going on under her nose. Zoe Hancock couldn't know what had transpired in the cabana and by the pool, but she would have to be as thick as a brick not to pick up on what was humming between James and his secretary. She had to know that the moment she left them alone together...

Lucy couldn't bear the thought of his mother knowing. Being here under the same roof and knowing. It wouldn't be private. Not emotionally private. And that felt horribly wrong to her.

James had said—*Don't let her interfere with this.*

But what was *this?*

If she was more than a lay for the night...if he really thought they were natural partners...that would still be true tomorrow.

She couldn't stay.

Not with his mother here.

It wouldn't feel right to her.

Dinner was over. Coffee had been served. Best she leave now while Zoe was still indulging herself with the chocolate mints she'd brought with the coffee. She stood up, determined on taking her leave, regardless of how deeply she was still aroused by the promise of *more* with James.

'It was a lovely dinner, Zoe. And a most enjoyable swim, James. But I really must be going now,' she rattled out, giving them both what felt like a glassy smile.

Surprise stamped on both their faces.

'If you'll excuse me...'

'Of course, dear, if you must,' Zoe graciously supplied.

'There's work tomorrow,' Lucy babbled and headed straight for the coat-stand where her handbag had been hung again on her return upstairs.

There was a scrape of chairs behind her, making her nerves leap in wild agitation.

'I'll see you out to your car,' James stated, and his firm tone brooked no opposition.

He said nothing more, not inside the house, nor on the climb up the flight of steps outside, but Lucy felt his dark brooding presence encompassing her, tugging on the sexual promise that was still wreaking its inner havoc, and her heart pounded with fearful uncertainties. Was she breaking something she should have stayed with?

She fumbled in her bag for the car-keys. It was too late to change her mind about going. Besides, she didn't want to. It *didn't* feel right with his mother there. And she wanted more than sex with James.

'Why are you running away?' came the harsh demand behind her.

'I'm not. I'll be at the office tomorrow,' she argued, reaching the driver's side of her car and almost flinging herself into the seat, anxious not to be stopped, not to be drawn into an embrace that could change her mind.

He closed the door for her and stood there, still gripping it. 'Then don't be late for work, Lucy,' he warned, an underlying threat of retribution in his tone.

She inserted the ignition key and looked up at him. His eyes were narrowed slits but she felt the force of the will behind them, fiercely probing and determined on a resolution that went *his* way.

'I'll be there...on time,' Lucy promised, then gunned the engine.

James nodded and stepped away.

She backed out of the parking slot and drove off, tremulously aware of her conflicting needs and James at the centre of them.

Tomorrow, she kept repeating to herself. Tomorrow she would have more answers to where she was heading with James Hancock. Nothing was predictable. Nothing was safe or sensible, either. Which probably meant she'd completely lost her mind.

Everything depended on *him*.

CHAPTER TWELVE

FOUR weeks...the four most wonderful, exhilarating, sensational, worth living for weeks she'd ever lived, Lucy reflected, even if there was a lifetime price to pay for it. Though she shouldn't think like that. Not yet. There was no sign at this point that James was getting the least bit bored with her, which left a possibility that their relationship might wear what she had to tell him.

The sex between them was still red-hot, invariably igniting an urgency that drove them to take wild chances, and even when they were concentrating on work, their desire for each other simmered around the edge of it, waiting to be satisfied again...and again...and again. In fact, Lucy didn't feel she belonged to herself any more. Everything she did, thought and felt was linked to James.

Which made today's decision not to fly to Melbourne with him a wrenching one, but she couldn't think about the future when they were together, and they were together so constantly, it was all too easy just to let herself be immersed in the excitement and pleasure of being with him, and put off dealing with what really did have to be faced.

A massive pile of washing and ironing to do, she'd pleaded to James. Which was true enough,

147

Lucy thought ironically, as she trudged up the stairs to her apartment. But it was the shocking and frightening knowledge of her pregnancy that she couldn't keep pushing aside. How it had happened, given she had not once missed taking her contraceptive pill, she had no idea, but a missed period and a pregnancy test had wiped out any doubt about it.

Maybe James was just so potent, he'd worn out her protection. She wished now that he'd kept on his practice of always using condoms. Though there was no point in thinking about *how* or *if only*. It was a done deed.

Her first impulse—after the shock of finding out—was to hide the fact from James and hang onto what she had with him for as long as she could. It felt as though she'd waited all her life for this one man, and still wanting him so much, she kept shying away from presenting him with the knowledge they'd made a baby.

It would change everything—whether for better or worse she didn't know and was too scared to lay it on the line.

Nevertheless, as much as she longed to hide her pregnancy and pretend nothing was different, a deeply rooted core of common sense insisted she couldn't keep holding such a huge secret from James, not when their relationship was so very intimate. Besides, the deception would inevitably play on her mind, spoiling things anyway. Somehow she had to decide what to do.

Sighing heavily, Lucy pushed open the door that

led from the stairwell to her floor. As usual it banged
shut behind her. Ahead of her she noticed the door
to Josh's apartment standing half-open, and wondered if it was an invitation to drop in. Being in no
mood to talk to anyone, she went no further than
her own apartment, feeling slightly guilty at the little
contact they'd had since Josh had helped re-vamp
her image.

'Ah! Caught you!' his voice rang out, halting her
as she was about to insert her key in the lock. 'The
intrepid sleuth strikes again!' he declared triumphantly.

It teased a smile from her as she turned to return
a greeting. 'Hi to you, too.'

He leaned against his door-jamb and surveyed
her, his eyebrows waggling above wickedly dancing
eyes. 'A little tired from constant romping with
James?'

'A house-keeping night,' she dryly replied, letting
him know it was not for socialising.

'But it *is* going well with him?'

'You could say that.' She was not about to dump
her current problem on Josh before thinking it
through herself.

'Your mother called,' he announced with more
waggling of eyebrows. 'You've neglected her dread-
fully. In fact, you're in the dog-house. She has called
and called and you are never home. She had to ring
me to find out if you were still alive.'

'Oh, hell!' Lucy muttered, sagging against
the wall.

'Bad, bad girl!' Josh mockingly chided. 'Nor have you been up to visit her for six weeks. Any minute now you're going to wear the label of the prodigal daughter.'

She grimaced, mentally hearing her mother rolling out these complaints to Josh. 'It's true,' she confessed. 'I've been totally selfish the past few weeks. And I didn't want to lie to her about what I've been doing so I just plain avoided it.'

He gave her a sympathetic look. 'Being in love is not a crime, Lucy love.'

'Oh, no? Risking my job by getting involved with my employer? My mother will have a field day on that one, let alone keeping the convertible and...' She bit down on the worst sin of all—getting pregnant outside of marriage.

'And?' Josh instantly prompted.

'Never mind.' She gave him a glum look. 'My crimes against common sense are legion at the moment.'

He adopted a stern headmaster pose, shaking his finger at her. 'Well, may I advise you...don't forget her birthday, which she let me know was this weekend, and if you don't call and grovel, and subsequently turn up with the fatted calf...'

'Mum's birthday!' Lucy smacked her forehead with the heel of her hand. 'Oh, Josh! I am awful!'

'Not at all. Intensely pre-occupied might cover it.'

'I'll go and call her right now.' She pushed herself off the wall, tossing him an apologetic wince. 'Thanks for catching me.'

He grinned. 'Just don't kill the messenger boy.'

It won an ironic laugh. 'You're safe, Josh.'

The safest person she knew, Lucy thought as she let herself into her own apartment. He never judged. He was there for her when she needed a friend. He listened and tried to help. But her current biggest problem was painfully private and not up for discussion...yet.

First things first, she told herself, heading for the telephone on the kitchen bench.

She had to talk to her mother.

Her mother...who had married the man who'd made her pregnant, a mistake in judgement that had scarred the rest of her life, all because of her need to be *respectable*. Though she would have hated the social blight of being an unmarried mother, which might have been just as scarring for her.

It had been different for Zoe Hancock. Respectability hadn't meant so much to her, not enough to marry a man who had only been a brief spark, not a lasting passion. She seemed to have taken being an unmarried mother in her stride...with a lot of help from the people James called honorary aunts and uncles.

Neither woman had considered an abortion and Lucy knew she wouldn't, either. She was twenty-eight years old and had no doubt in her heart there would never be another James. Whatever his response to her pregnancy, she would have the baby and keep it. But she desperately wanted to be the lasting passion in James' life.

Four weeks...it really wasn't enough time to be sure this was a rock-solid relationship to James. He had never talked about *love*. What if his passion for her reached burn-out before she was even visibly pregnant?

Should she wait, holding her secret from him until she was as sure as she could be that she was the only woman he would ever want, not just the sexiest woman he'd ever met up until now?

Yet if he truly felt they were natural partners...

Lucy shook her head.

It was all so terribly risky, whichever way she looked at it.

And she had to call her mother.

Four weeks, James reflected, claiming his Porsche from the airport car-park and happily eager to drive to the office and get back to Lucy. Best four weeks of his life, he decided. Not one falling out with Lucy over work or play, and she suited him brilliantly in both areas.

In fact, the trip to Melbourne had been a drag without her. He'd missed her company—missed her comments on the client and situation he'd had to deal with, missed her smiles and the sparkle of shared understanding in her eyes. And the hotel bed would definitely have provided more comfort and satisfaction—not to mention pleasure—with her in it.

What they had together was great. No doubt about it. Even the sluggish pace of the traffic into the city could not fray his good mood this morning. It gave him more time to plan what he'd do with Lucy over the coming weekend. For once, he was entirely free of work and social commitments. They could do anything they fancied. James entertained himself with various highly desirable fancies all the way to the office.

And there she was, waiting for him, saucily sexy in a little scarlet shift with a gold chain belt dangling provocatively around her hips. Her green eyes had that look of eating him up which always excited him, and even as a grin of sheer pleasure broke across his face, he could feel himself stirring, wanting the more intense pleasure of connecting physically with her.

'How did it go in Melbourne?' she asked.

His office, he decided.

'Everything settled,' he assured her, not the least bit interested in going into details.

With his briefcase occupying one hand—something he had to get rid of—he hooked his free arm around Lucy, drawing her with him as he headed for the connecting door and his larger, more comfortable, more private office. It felt so good, having her at his side again.

'All washed and ironed?' he teased.

'Enough to go on with,' she answered wryly.

'Good. Because I have big plans for us this weekend.'

He felt her body tensing. It alerted him to a problem even before she stopped, momentarily halting the purpose burning in his mind. Her face turned up to his, her eyes filled with an eloquent appeal for understanding.

'I can't be with you this weekend, James,' she said, the decision clearly paining her.

'Why not?' he asked, trying to sound reasonable against a rush of frustration.

'I have to go home. To Gosford, I mean.'

'Visiting your mother?'

'Yes. It's been six weeks and...'

'It's okay.' Not what he'd fancied, but he could ride with it. 'I'll go with you. I don't mind meeting your mother. You've met mine.'

'No!' she cried, showing clear signs of agitation. 'I mean...it's just not appropriate this weekend, James. It's her birthday.'

'So?'

He frowned over her obvious reluctance to introduce him to her mother. What was the problem? Why was she acting so oddly, floundering in the face of his perfectly logical question.

'It's a mother/daughter thing. We always celebrate her birthday together,' she babbled, actually wringing her hands.

His gut told him it was more than this. 'Which day is your mother's birthday?' he asked, needing to get to the bottom of what was really going on.

'Tomorrow. But I've got my bag packed and in the car, and I'll be leaving straight after work. My mother has already made plans, James, expecting me to fall in with them, so I'll have to spend the whole weekend with her.'

There was an anxious appeal in her eyes that begged him not to interfere, not to make any claims on her. It clicked through his mind that she'd cried off going to Melbourne and now she wanted another two days without him. After four weeks of very mutual intimacy, why this? Then it hit him. Four weeks...

He heaved a relieved sigh as understanding cleared his concerns. Lucy was funny about some things...like being embarrassed about his mother knowing they were having sex together. Never mind that his mother was completely blasé about her own affairs! *And* she so clearly approved of Lucy as a partner for him, taking her out to lunches and showing her all her favourite shopping places in Balmain.

Good thing the chicken pox scare was over and she'd flown back to Melbourne. He preferred to have Lucy to himself. But since Lucy had been so good about *his* mother's foibles, it was only fair for him to give consideration to *her* mother.

He dropped his briefcase and turned to draw her into a reassuring embrace. She came stiffly, confirming his conclusion that sex was out for a few days. He gave her a soothing smile.

'It's okay. You don't have to be embarrassed about saying you've got your period. I am aware of a woman's cycle.'

A flood of heat swept into her cheeks. She dipped her head, her long lashes veiling her eyes. Clearly she was *acutely* embarrassed. Did she think he would have wanted sex anyway, not respecting her feelings?

'I'd prefer it if you're open with me, Lucy, not hiding anything,' he gently chided.

She bit her lips. Sensing a strong inner turmoil he didn't understand at all, James decided to let the issue drop for the moment, not wanting her to be upset. 'Hey...' He tenderly tilted her chin. 'It's no big deal. Just having your company is great to me.'

Her lashes lifted and the anguished uncertainty that poured out at him gave James a severe jolt. She couldn't think all he wanted her for was sex...could she? Admittedly he could barely keep his hands off her, but she'd been just as hot and hungry. Definitely *mutual* desire! So what was going on here? Did she only want *him* for sex?

Perplexed, disturbed, James retreated to familiar ground. 'Let's get on with work. Okay?' He released her, picked up his briefcase and proceeded to dump it on his desk. 'Any e-mails that need urgent answering this morning?' he tossed at her.

'I'll get the print-outs,' she answered and fled like a cat on a hot tin roof.

James sat in his chair, feeling like a pricked balloon, all his earlier good humour totally evaporated. He'd dealt successfully with people for too many years not to know something was very wrong here. Lucy's behaviour did not add up to what he felt could be reasonably expected of their relationship.

She enjoyed his company. He knew she did.

No-one could fake the instinctively positive response he saw in her eyes, the easy rapport in their conversations, the body language that openly expressed pleasure in being with him. There had to be some other factor at play here, something more than being funny about her period.

Her mother?

Was Lucy holding some secret she didn't want to reveal about her mother?

Further thought reminded him of Lucy's discomfort when his own mother had started boring in about family background. Of course, no-one liked being so obviously cross-examined. All the same, Lucy had never brought up the subject of her mother herself—no reference at all to her life in Gosford—until now. And that was an unusual omission, given that most women did mention family, if only in passing.

His mind was revolving around this intriguing little mystery when Lucy re-entered his office, carrying the e-mail print-outs. He hadn't even opened his briefcase, but getting to work was not his priority here. Seeing that Lucy still looked tense, he leaned back in his chair, promoting a relaxed mood, and offered a friendly smile.

'I was just thinking...I don't even know your mother's name. I presume it's *something* Worthington,' he prompted.

'Ruth. It's Ruth Worthington,' she replied stiffly.

'And where in Gosford does she live?'

Lucy frowned, not welcoming this line of questioning. 'Green Point,' she bit out.

Not giving an actual address, James noted. 'Well, I wondered—' he pressed on '—would Ruth *mind* having me as a guest this weekend? I mean...does she disapprove of our relationship?'

Her feet instantly faltered. Her cheeks bloomed with hot colour again. 'It's a small house. It doesn't have a guest room.'

And there'd be no sleeping with her under her mother's roof, James instantly deduced.

'Besides,' she went on with a telling grimace, 'I haven't even told her I won the car yet. And I haven't told her about—' she took a deep breath '—about us.'

James had the strong impression that 'us' was a huge hurdle to be negotiated, and why anyone would hold back the news of winning such a car was a puzzle in itself. The mystery deepened.

'Might be easier just to present her with the lot in one shot,' he suggested, undeterred by the image of a dragon lady.

'No...' She shook her head, dropping her gaze from his, nervously fingering the pages in her hands. 'That wouldn't work at all well. Believe me—' another deep breath and her gaze lifted reluctantly, appealing for his forebearance '—I have to go and it's best I go alone. I'm sorry to...to disappoint you, but that's how it is.'

'Okay. It was just a thought,' he said dismissively, irony tilting his smile. 'I didn't know I was a deep, dark secret.'

Her chin lifted. 'You won't be after this weekend,' she promised with an odd intonation—like a mixture of pride and pain.

Was there some old private conflict with her mother she didn't want to share?

'Good!' he said, approving her decision to be open with her mother, if not with him. Though he didn't intend for that situation to continue much longer, either. 'Then I'll look forward to meeting your mother another time.'

'I hope so,' she muttered, resuming her walk to his desk, holding out the e-mails for his attention. 'These came in.'

Still he sensed turmoil in her mind. He thought about pursuing the subject, but decided it would not win him anything. Lucy's mind was made up and he sensed there'd be no changing it. But she wasn't happy about this trip back to the maternal home. She was expecting conflict.

James pondered the situation throughout the day, remembering how he'd accused Lucy of putting her life into neat little pockets. She'd broken that rule with him, but clearly there were other pockets which were still buttoned up. Why, was the question. What drove a young woman to divide up her life as Lucy did? What was the mystery about her mother?

She begged off lunch with him, saying she had to buy a birthday gift. The mission neatly avoided an opportunity for personal chat. It grew more and more obvious as the afternoon wore on that she was in a fraught, distracted state. Concern for her safety on the road drove him to suggest she leave early to beat the peak-hour traffic.

'You don't mind?' she asked anxiously, gesturing at the papers on his desk. 'We're not finished.'

'Leave it to me. Go on,' he urged.

She hesitated, eyeing him uncertainly. 'I am sorry about this weekend.'

'Can't be helped.' He shrugged and moved to give her shoulders a light, reassuring squeeze. 'Take care driving. I want you back here safe and sound on Monday. Okay?'

'Yes,' she whispered shakily.

He bent and planted a gentle kiss on her mouth.

She barely responded, breaking away quickly. 'Thanks, James,' she breathed on a ragged sigh, and was off.

One way or another, he was going to find out what was in this pocket which was being kept so tightly buttoned. Lucy might not consider her family situation *his* business, but he was going to make it his business. Something was wrong and it needed to be put right.

Apart from which, secrets were bad. They showed a lack of trust. They formed barriers to the intimacy he'd thought he had with Lucy. Those barriers had to be broken down. Right from the beginning he'd wanted to know Lucy Worthington inside out, and having come this far, he wasn't about to be stopped.

Not by anything!

CHAPTER THIRTEEN

LUCY managed to concentrate enough to get the car and herself over the harbour bridge and into the right lane that would take her north to the central coast. All she had to do then was virtually follow the car in front of her, which was just as well, because she was in a tangle of torment over letting James believe she had her period.

Her period! What a black joke that was! It had been on the tip of her tongue to tell him the truth. All day she had wavered over revealing her pregnancy or keeping it hidden. In the end, the lure of having him as her lover for another month overrode her conscience. She just couldn't risk a negative reaction. Not yet.

And he wouldn't guess the truth, not believing her monthly cycle was running as it normally would. By Monday she might get over feeling sick about the deceit. James would think her period was over and hopefully they would go on as before...if she could keep pushing her condition to the back of her mind. In her present mental state, that was a big *if.*

At least he hadn't pressed her too much about this weekend with her mother. He'd really been kind about letting her go early, too. Kind and considerate. Like he truly did care about her. Combining that with his assurance this morning that he enjoyed her company, with or without sex…maybe she could tell him the truth without everything blowing up in her face.

The torment of uncertainty continued while the car took her away from Sydney. She wasn't aware of having crossed the Hawkesbury Bridge and the big dipper of the Mooney Mooney Bridge—landmarks along the expressway. It was a jolt when she saw the exit sign to Gosford. It forcefully reminded her she would soon be facing her mother and she'd better get herself ready to fend off the criticisms that were bound to be aimed at her.

'What train will you be on?' she'd been asked last night.

'You won't have to meet a train. I'll be coming by car, Mum,' she'd answered, steeling herself to argue her way past her mother's concept of a sensible car.

'Well, if Josh is giving you a lift, you just tell him he'd better get you here safely in that dreadful old sports car of his. And he's not to roar into my driveway like a larrikin.'

The steel wilted. 'Josh is not a larrikin, Mum. And he's always been safe.'

Safe, safe, safe… Lucy mocked savagely to herself as she took the Gosford exit. Having flouted all the *safe* rules, she was now looking right down the barrel of the consequences. Which, of course, her mother had warned her about. Compared to falling pregnant to her boss with no marriage in view, showing up in a red Alpha Spider convertible and shocking her mother with it was the least of her worries.

Though the brief sense of cavalier bravado took an abrupt dive when she spotted her mother watering the garden and caught the astonished look on her face as the Alpha turned into the driveway with *her daughter* in the driver's seat. Lucy switched off the ignition and sat for several moments, trying to raise her sinking heart.

'What on earth are you doing in that car and why are you driving it?' came her mother's shrill demands.

Taking a deep breath, Lucy hauled herself out of the red sports convertible, shut the door, and stood beside it, her hand gripping it in a show of proud possession. 'I'm driving it because it's mine. I won it in a raffle.' She beamed a smile full of teeth at her mother. 'Big surprise!'

Ruth Worthington gaped—first at Lucy, then at the car, and back at Lucy, who'd forgotten she'd changed her style of dress in the turmoil of everything else. 'A raffle,' she said weakly, clearly not knowing what to make of anything yet.

'Isn't it great? It's an Alpha Spider, an Italian sports car, and I've christened it Orlando,' Lucy burbled on, projecting unquenchable enthusiasm. 'You know, Mum, I've never won anything in my entire life, and to win this...' She released the door to make an expansive gesture. 'It was so unbelievable I'm still getting used to it.'

And her mother would take even longer to get used to it. If ever. Oddly enough, Lucy found herself not caring. Josh was right. It was *her life*.

Ruth Worthington would only be forty-seven tomorrow but somehow she'd made herself sexless, wearing no-nonsense clothes and having her greying, salt and pepper hair cut in a short layered style that required no more than a quick comb through it. She was even wearing grey—flat-heeled grey shoes, grey skirt, grey and white tailored blouse —and if she chose to live a grey life, well that was her choice, but it wasn't going to be Lucy's, no matter how things worked out with James.

A wave of belligerent self-assertion lifted her chin at her mother's continued silence. Judgements were undoubtedly being made and any second now they would start raining down on Lucy's head. She could only hope some kind of truce could be drawn so the birthday weekend wasn't a complete disaster.

'You know, you've worn glasses since you were in primary school,' her mother mused with a little shake of her head. 'You look quite lovely without them, Lucy.'

The soft comment was so unexpected—and nice—Lucy ended up grinning. 'I finally decided to get contact lenses.'

'It makes a real difference to your face. And your red dress... I didn't realise... I would never have dressed you in red...but red suits you. Especially with your hair down and fluffed out.'

Lucy's heart suddenly soared. To get compliments, not criticism…it was almost as unbelievable as winning the car. 'How about putting down that garden hose so I can give you a birthday hug?'

Her mother actually laughed. 'Well, you certainly have given me a big surprise.'

The hose, of course, couldn't just be dropped. The garden tap had to be turned off. Long-time habits weren't discarded in one fell swoop, but her mother did move briskly and her arms were open, ready to hug her daughter back when Lucy met her halfway between the car and the tap.

'It's lovely to see you, dear,' she murmured, then pulled slightly away to offer a wry little smile. 'I'm sorry I was so put out on the phone last night, but I've missed your calls and when I couldn't reach you, I had a silly, panicky sense I was losing you.'

'You'll always be my Mum,' Lucy reassured her on a rush of guilt. 'I've just been caught up in lots of things lately.'

'So I see.' A few wise nods. 'Well, let's have a look at this prize you've won. Does driving…Orlando…?' She looked totally bemused at a car having been personalised with a name. 'Make you feel like a million dollars?'

'Yes, it does,' Lucy answered, surprised into impulsively suggesting, 'Hop in, Mum, and I'll take you for a spin around the block. Best way of showing you what it's like.'

She hesitated. 'The house is unlocked.'

'We'll only be a few minutes.'

'But…'

'Take a risk,' Lucy recklessly advised.

And to her further surprise, always-play-safe Ruth Worthington actually did, proceeding to settle herself somewhat gingerly in the low passenger seat.

It was only a short ride but her mother seemed to enjoy it, smiling at Lucy as the wind ruffled her hair. When they returned to the house, she got out and said thoughtfully, 'It gives you a sense of freedom, doesn't it?'

Lucy laughed, amazed and delighted she was getting such an open-minded response. 'And a bit of zip in my life.'

'Not too much zip, I hope. Speeding is not sensible.'

'I've been watching that I don't. The car has a cruise control button to save me from going over the speed limit on the expressway, even accidentally.'

'Good!' She waited until Lucy had collected her bag and they were walking to the house, then archly asked, 'So who is the man?'

'What man?'

It earned a dry look. 'I might be one year older tomorrow, but I'm not senile, Lucy. Everything adds up to a new man in your life. And I'm happy for you. After all, you are twenty-eight.'

'Mmmh...' A safe, non-committal reply.

'You can tell me all about him after you put your things in your room,' her mother invited with an indulgent smile.

Not *all* about him, Lucy darkly decided. Her mother didn't deserve to have her birthday ruined.

And she'd been so nice about the car, even seeming to understand why Lucy had kept it instead of trading it in. Although she didn't have the whole picture—the motivating force being the need to impress James with a new exciting image. Lucy wasn't sure how much of the picture—featuring James—could be given before disapproval kicked in.

She was trying to calculate this as she unpacked her bag and put away her clothes. The wretched weight of the deceit she had allowed to stay in place with James today crept up on her and it was suddenly very clear that she couldn't go through with deceiving her mother about anything. She would hold back about her pregnancy for a while, but not about James being her boss, nor how much the relationship meant to her.

She wanted her mother to understand, needed her to be supportive. That was probably expecting too much, but…what was their relationship worth if she couldn't confide her love for a man and hope for a sympathetic ear? Maybe it was weak of her but she was tired of being independent, working everything out for herself. Josh was a good friend—the best of friends—and being able to lean on his shoulder was a big help…but she really wanted her mother.

Tears pricked her eyes and she hurriedly blinked them away. Silly to get all wet about it. Nevertheless, if there was ever a time to confide, this was it, and Lucy headed out to the kitchen, determined to lay out the truth…except for the pregnancy bit.

However, in the hours of chat that followed, Lucy did do a bit of judicious editing—the very private stuff—although she could see her mother mentally filling in the blanks. To her deep relief, while a few worried frowns occurred here and there, no criticism came at all.

'You're very much in love with him, aren't you?' It was more a statement than a question, accompanied by a look that seemed to understand everything.

Lucy had to blink hard. 'Yes, I am,' she answered huskily. 'I was strongly attracted to him all along. I really lived to go to work, Mum. It's more so now.'

She nodded. 'And James...does he love you, Lucy?'

'He hasn't said so...but it *feels* like that.'

'Well, I hope it will turn out right for you.' She paused, reservations creeping into her eyes. 'I don't want to be a wet blanket, Lucy. It's lovely to see you all bright and beautiful and glowing with love. But...have you considered...'

'What if it turns out wrong?' Lucy said the dread words for her—the same words that resided in her heart, causing it to ache with uncertainty.

Her mother sighed ruefully. 'Sometimes these office affairs don't last. It's easy to fall into them...proximity. But you have such a close working relationship with James, I think your position would become untenable if he...decided he'd had enough and wanted to take up with someone else.'

Pain sliced through her. He couldn't go from her to another Buffy. It would kill her.

'What would you do, Lucy? Where would you go?' her mother pressed worriedly.

'I don't want to think about that. Not until I have to,' Lucy rushed out vehemently. 'I don't want to be negative, Mum,' she appealed.

'Of course not,' came the quick, soothing reply. 'It was only with James being your boss...'

'I know. And he considered that, too, holding back for a long time.' *Until she looked sexy.* Lucy shook off the disturbing doubt and clutched at a positive point, rushing it out. 'He wanted to come and meet you this weekend...'

'Well, that's a good sign.'

'Yes. Yes, it is,' Lucy fiercely told herself, more than answering her mother.

'Is he coming?'

'No. I put him off. It's your birthday and...'

'You hadn't told me about him.'

'I couldn't just land him on you, Mum.'

She nodded. 'You were worried about my response.'

'It wouldn't have been fair...to either of you. And we always spend your birthday together. I told him another time would be better.'

She smiled. 'I'll look forward to meeting him.'

Would there be another time?

Her mother was being so...*accepting*...somehow it made the deception about her pregnancy more wrong than ever!

Her desperate need for James might carry her through fooling him for a while longer, but...it was her mother who would still be here for her if things went wrong with him. That was the bottom-line truth she didn't want to look at. Nevertheless, it was a truth she couldn't ignore.

It played on her mind all through the rest of Friday night and Saturday, despite every effort to put a happy face on everything for her mother's birthday. She knew, on Sunday morning, she couldn't carry this burden any longer. They had shared a late breakfast and were sitting over coffee when Lucy finally took the plunge.

'Mum…' She lifted eyes filled with anguished appeal. 'I didn't want to tell you…but I can't *not* tell you…'

A frown of puzzled concern. 'What is it, Lucy?'

She hunted desperately for some not so shocking way to say it, but there was no escape to be found in words. Her stomach was a churning mess. Her heart felt as though it was in a vise. There was an almost impassable lump in her throat. Just spill out the truth, her mind screamed. Get it over with.

'I'm pregnant.'

Right before her eyes she saw her mother's face sag, age, her whole expression emptying of any pleasure in life. It was worse than anything she had anticipated. And Lucy was helpless to make it better. There was nothing she could say, nothing she could do.

The sin—the very same sin that had led to bad consequences in her mother's life—filled the silence stretching between them, making it heavier, loading it with guilt and shame and an escalating mountain of regrets for not taking heed, for choosing a wild, reckless path that tossed risks aside. There was no point in saying she had used contraception. Pregnant was pregnant, and excuses were useless.

The doorbell rang, making them both jerk out of the pall of memories. Her mother shook her head, frowned, then scraped her chair back.

'Are you expecting someone?' Lucy blurted out.

'Probably Jean from next door.' Her eyes were sick, her voice dull. 'She wanted some geranium cuttings. I'll tell her to take them.'

She pushed herself up and moved slowly towards the door into the hallway, like a sleep walker in the middle of a nightmare.

Lucy closed her eyes, buried her head in her hands, and waited.

CHAPTER FOURTEEN

THEY had to be at home, James assured himself, waiting for the doorbell to be answered. Lucy's car was in the driveway. It had made it easy for him to pick out the right house, although he'd also checked that the address matched the one he'd found in the telephone book. He looked with satisfaction at his Porsche, now parked behind the red convertible. The Alpha was blocked in, which gave him a negotiating position with this visit.

All the same, if Lucy and her mother were inside, they were slow to open the door. He thought about giving the button another press, then decided the bell must have been heard the first time. It *was* a small house. Very neat and tidy and scrupulously maintained. So was the garden and lawn. Ruth Worthington undoubtedly had a tidy mind, everything having to be just right and in its place.

Lucy was like that in her work. She used to dress like that, too, all neatly pinned and buttoned. James was pondering her mother's influence—and wondering what else he would discover today—when he heard the metallic click of the door being opened. He hastily composed a bright happy expression, smile hovering, persuasive patter ready to roll off his tongue.

He'd hoped it would be Lucy, but it wasn't, and the woman he was suddenly facing looked ill and defeated by the illness. Something life-threatening? James thought, and instantly regretted the urge that had driven him here, intruding on what could be a seriously private time between mother and daughter. Lucy's stress was easily answered if what he guessed was the case and she'd just found out about it—something badly wrong.

The woman looked blankly at him—washed out grey-green eyes. Despite her obvious suffering, her short greying hair was neatly combed and she was quite smartly dressed in navy slacks and a white and navy striped top. Appearances meant a lot to her, James thought, and savagely wished he'd waited until Lucy was ready to introduce him to her mother.

Too late now. He couldn't cry off with some lame excuse of coming to the wrong house. Sooner or later a meeting would be arranged and she might remember him. He had to go through with his plan, adapting it to the circumstances.

'Mrs Worthington?' he asked, making identification certain.

'Yes. Who are you? What do you want?' Her voice was flat, slow, disinterested, and he could see it was difficult for her to focus on a stranger's needs.

'My name is James Hancock. Your daughter...'

'James Hancock?' It was as though his name had snapped her back to life, her eyes suddenly sharp and piercing.

'Yes. I was...'

'The man Lucy works for?'

'Yes.'

'Did Lucy invite you here today?'

'No. But we are *more* than business associates, Mrs Worthington, and I thought…'

'Yes. Much more,' she retorted, with a ferocity of feeling that knocked James back on his heels. 'And I think you'd better come in because my daughter has something to tell you, and I want to see for myself what kind of man you are, James Hancock.'

It was a facade-stripping challenge that couldn't be refused by any man worth his salt and it spun James' mind right around. Gone were any thoughts of illness. Ruth Worthington had just been transformed into a fire-eating dragon lady and James was already sharpening his own weapons to fight for Lucy as he stepped forward.

'Thank you. I'd like to come in and hear what Lucy has to tell me,' he said, all his aggressive and protective instincts flooding to the fore.

Ruth Worthington stood back and let him in, her shoulders squared now, very upright and unyielding in her stance. James paused in the hall, giving her time to shut the door and precede him to wherever Lucy was. She marched down the hall ahead of him, obviously prepared to seize the fighting ground and make it hers.

James followed, determined not to be outplayed by what he now perceived as very definitely *the enemy*. Something *was* very wrong here and he was intent on rescuing Lucy from it. No mother had the right to dominate or screw up her daughter's life. Lucy felt free with him. She had every right to freedom of choice.

They entered a kitchen. Lucy sat slumped over a table, head in her hands, a picture of despairing dejection. Whatever had been going here, it was going to stop right now!

'Lucy?' he called, demanding her attention.

Her hands flew away from her face as she jerked it towards him, shock widening her eyes and parting her lips. 'James?' It was an incredulous whisper.

'I figured you needed some support and I'm here to give it,' he declared.

'Support?' she echoed, seemingly unable to take in his offer or what it meant.

'Well, we'll soon see about that,' Ruth Worthington said in a harsh, judgemental tone, raising James' hackles even further. 'Tell him, Lucy. Either you tell him or I will.'

It was an uncompromising threat, and Lucy turned to her mother, clearly appalled by it and desperately seeking some other course. 'Mum, it's...it's my decision,' she pleaded, her hands turning palm upwards in painful eloquence.

James seethed at the torment her mother was putting her through. 'You don't have to take her orders, Lucy,' he insisted vehemently.

Ruth Worthington ignored him, still holding Lucy's attention despite his strong assertion. 'I won't have you living in a fool's paradise as I did,' she said, surprising him with a complete change of

tone. Determination was tempered by a note of anguished sympathy, and her hands made their own
agitated appeal. 'You *must* tell him, Lucy. Then
you'll know.'

Feeling somewhat confused by this new twist,
James decided he agreed with her. 'I think that's a
good idea. Then I'll know, too. The sooner, the better.'

A fool's paradise…

The words sliced into Lucy's heart and cut out
any lingering temptation to carry on some deceit
with James. They sliced into her mind, clearing it
of the fog of desire that four weeks of unbridled lust
had built up. Four weeks—only a month—but
there'd been eight months of working together before that. James had more than long enough to know
what he felt about her and how important she was
to his life.

She gathered herself together and stood up. The
flash of proud approval in her mother's eyes
strengthened her will to face James with the truth.
She straightened her shoulders, knowing she was not
alone, whatever happened. Her mother would stand
by her.

James stood proud and tall, too, at the other end
of the table. His vivid blue eyes were blazing at her,
projecting a fierce command to explain what was
going on. He wore casual clothes—red sports shirt,
cream slacks—and his male animal sex appeal
seemed to be heightened by the tension in the room.

A warrior come to do battle, Lucy thought—big, indomitable and determined to win.

It made her feel very small, very vulnerable, very frightened of losing. Her frantic mind clutched at what he'd said a few moments ago—*he'd come to give her support.* Please let it be true, she prayed, though she didn't really know what he meant by it or what had brought him here. All she knew was she had to say it, so she forced out the fateful words.

'I'm pregnant.'

'Pregnant?' he echoed dazedly, disbelief and confusion chasing across his face. He shook his head. 'But you said...'

'No, I didn't, James. You assumed I had my period and I...' Shame burned her cheeks. She swallowed hard, working some moisture into her dry mouth. 'I let you because...'

'How can you be pregnant?' he cut in, looking bewildered. 'You said...you were safe.'

Safe, safe, safe... was that word going to mock her forever?

A tide of violent emotion swept through Lucy, spilling out a torrent of her own torment. 'I swear to you I didn't mess up the contraception. I never missed a pill. Every morning without fail I took it, so it's not my fault. You...I...we...' She faltered, losing the plot.

'You're blaming me?' he asked with a wry twist of his mouth.

Out of the whirl of her mind shot the one and only cause for failure she'd thought of. 'You're just too sexy, James Hancock. And obviously very potent. *Too* potent.'

'What?'

His stunned expression churned Lucy into a further wild indiscretion. 'You know perfectly well what I mean and don't you deny it!'

'Oh, I won't.' He shook his head. 'No way would I deny my part in getting you pregnant. Seems to me you're the one who's been in denial.' He frowned at her. 'Is this what you were so uptight about on Friday?'

Denial...deceit...in wretched shame Lucy offered the only excuse she had. 'I didn't know how you'd take it.'

'Lucy...' His tone was gently chiding. The frown disappeared and a smile started spreading across his face. 'So you're mostly upset because it wasn't planned.'

'No. Yes. I just didn't know if...well, I *didn't* know how you'd take it, James,' she finished helplessly.

'A baby...' He started grinning. 'This is bound to be one really special kid, being conceived against the odds.' Then he was coming around the table towards her, still grinning. 'We're going to have a baby.'

It was Lucy's turn to be stunned. Could she believe the pleasure he was emanating? 'Yes. Yes, we are,' she affirmed somewhat breathlessly.

'I know you like to feel in control of things, Lucy, but I guess nature decided on working a little miracle for us, and now that it's happened...it doesn't really matter, does it?'

Her turn to be bewildered. 'Doesn't it?'

'Not a bit,' he answered, his eyes glowing warm assurance at her. 'Just means we've got to get our heads around being parents now instead of in the future.'

'Future?' she echoed.

He reached out and curled his hands around her shoulders, his thumbs fanning her collar-bones as his gaze locked onto hers with commanding intensity, searing away any doubts she might be nursing.

'You surely didn't imagine I was going to let you move out of my life.' His voice purred into her mind and stroked her heart. 'A partner like you?' He smiled, projecting all the confidence in the world. 'We were made for each other, Lucy.'

Still she couldn't quite take in what was happening. 'You don't mind...about the baby?'

'You and I...we make the best kind of magic, Lucy. Why shouldn't we expect miraculous things to occur when we're together?' His eyes sparkled, seeming to dance with happy thoughts. 'However we did it, we've made a baby and I think it's great.'

'You do?'

'I sure do,' he replied with resounding certainty. 'And since we're here with your mother—' he shot the judge of this situation a hard, challenging look, then softened his expression for Lucy '—we can start planning the wedding right now.'

'Wedding?' Lucy was beginning to feel like a fish out of water, gaping and gasping.

'We are definitely getting married before our baby is born,' he declared with determined intent.

'I don't think that's a good idea,' Lucy instantly protested, casting an agonised look at her mother. 'It…it didn't work for Mum, getting married because she fell pregnant with me.'

'Ah!' James said as though suddenly enlightened with a wealth of understanding. He shot a venomous look at her mother, then increased the pressure of his hands as his eyes bored into Lucy's. 'It didn't work for me, not having a father I could call my own,' he said forcefully. 'I will not be shunted off, Lucy. And I won't let you take *my* mother's path.'

'I don't want to,' she cried, suddenly seeing where he was coming from. Concern for his child was the focus here, not her. 'But there's more to marriage than getting tied together because of a baby, James.'

'We're tied together now,' he argued. 'As intimately as two people could be.'

'It's only been a month. What if…'

'A month? What do you call all the time you were with me before that—almost a year—fitting together like hand and glove in our work…'

'While you went to bed with other women,' she accused hotly.

'I didn't want to lose you. If I'd laid a hand on you at work…or even made suggestive remarks…how was I supposed to know you wouldn't have accused me of sexual harassment and walked out in high dudgeon?'

'You went with those women because of *me?* Is that what you're saying?'

'Distraction. I *told* you that.'

'How can I believe you? How can I know I'm not just the latest on the scoreboard? What if I risked marrying you, only to find you seeking *distraction* afterwards?'

'Dammit, Lucy! You're the total count. The perfect number for me. Why would I even *look* anywhere else?'

'You've never said that before.'

'Well, I'm saying it now.'

'Because of the baby...'

'No! I'm saying it because it's true.' He heaved an exasperated sigh. 'Why are you going on like this? You know we're perfect together. Nothing could be better. Don't you *feel* that?'

He looked as if he wanted to shake her until she admitted it. Lucy bit her lips. He was talking about sex and work, but there'd been no mention made of love.

'There's no risk, Lucy,' he declared emphatically.

She made a decision. 'If you still want to marry me *after* I have the baby...'

'Oh, no you don't!' He glowered at her through narrowed eyes. 'You're not stringing me along like you did Josh Rogan—now I want you, now I don't.'

'What?' her mother squawked. 'Josh?' her voice climbed incredulously.

'That's past history!' James shot at her. 'And not to be nagged over.'

'But...' she looked at Lucy.

There was no time for explanations. James was focused back on her, compelling her undivided attention, pouring out vehement passion.

'I'm here to stay, Lucy, and you'd better get used to it. You're *my* woman, and this is *my* child, and we're going to stick together because nothing else makes sense, and you ought to know that!'

It sounded good, weakening her doubts and bolstering her hopes. She heaved a rueful sigh as she confessed, 'Josh has never been more than a friend to me. He's *gay*. He was just doing me a favour, going to the ball with me because you thought I'd bring someone boring.'

James frowned disbelief. 'That guy... *gay?*'

'Yes.'

He let out his breath in a whoosh and relaxed into a wry smile. 'Lucy, *boring* I might have been able to deal with, but that guy tipped me over the edge. Be damned if I was going to let any other man have you!'

He released her shoulders and cupped her face, searching her eyes for the response he wanted. 'I love you, Lucy Worthington.' His voice was soft and tender. 'I love you through and through. There's not one bit about you I don't love. I drove up here today because I was worried about you. You seemed so stressed on Friday and I thought you must have some problem with your mother. I wanted to fix it for you. I want to make everything right for you. Don't you see? I *love* you.'

She was utterly transfixed by the words he spoke, words that seemed to be pulled from his heart and reflected in the deep blue pools of his eyes. Before she could form any reply there was a loud throat-clearing by her mother. James reacted instantly, an arm shooting around Lucy's shoulders to hug her to his side as he turned them both to face the woman he saw as his opponent.

'Mrs Worthington, this is *our* life...mine and Lucy's. And our child's,' he declared with ringing conviction. 'Whatever your own experience was, this is different and I'd be obliged if you keep right out of it.'

Different...Lucy almost wept at the stand James was making for her—it touched her so deeply. Could she dare to believe it would truly be different? Blissfully different? She let herself luxuriate in the warm security of his hug...the warm *loving* security. It felt so good. So right. Surely it had to be right. She looked at her mother, silently pleading for ver-ification, for support.

This isn't a fool's paradise, is it?

But her mother wasn't looking at her. Her gaze was fixed on James, still assessing him, weighing his words, his actions. A smile started to tug at her mouth. 'Make it Ruth,' she invited.

'Fine!' James said, seizing the advantage it seemed to give. 'I hope you like what you see, but if you don't, I'm going to have Lucy as my wife anyway. As soon as I can persuade her to marry me.'

Her mother's expression softened further as she looked at Lucy, then back to him. 'I don't think you're going to have to do much persuasion. My daughter was afraid of losing you, and that's not a good basis for marriage, James.'

'She'd have to run a long, long way to lose me, Ruth, and even then I'd chase her,' he retorted vehemently.

She nodded and gave Lucy a smile that seemed to brim with inner joy for her. 'I don't think it's a risk, darling. He *does* love you.'

'You're...you're okay with this, Mum?' Lucy barely got out over the lump in her throat.

'You weren't a fool...anywhere along the line,' came the soft acknowledgement. 'Your instincts were right, and you were right to follow them. Sometimes...not to risk...defeats what you really want. And true love is worth any risk.'

Lucy couldn't speak. Never before had her mother shown such intimate understanding. Tears misted her eyes as she realised that maybe she'd never given her mother the chance to...until now.

'I think I'm going to like you, Ruth,' James declared with a decisive infusion of warmth.

She raised an eyebrow at him but her eyes were actually twinkling. 'I've got some work to do in the garden. It may take an hour or so. Let me know when you've made Lucy feel confident of a happy future with you, and we *will* plan a wedding.'

James grinned back at her. 'Now I know where Lucy got that cut-you-off-at-the-knees sensible streak from. Thanks, Ruth.'

'I'll look forward to seeing you work some more miracles, James,' she retorted good-humouredly, sailing off to leave them alone together.

Lucy took a deep breath to relieve the tightness in her chest, turned to James, flung her arms around his neck and buried her face in the comforting flesh-warmth at the base of his throat. 'I'm sorry I couldn't tell you,' she whispered.

He gathered her body closer, his hands caressing her in possessive yearning as he tenderly rubbed his cheek against her hair. 'You can share everything with me, Lucy. Don't ever be afraid to say what's on your mind...in your heart.''

Released from all inhibitions, she gratefully gave him her heart. 'I love you, too, James. I just didn't know...how deep it went with you.'

'How about soulmate? Will that do?' he softly teased.

'Yes.'

His chest rose and fell, emitting a long sigh. 'It's going to be good...having a baby...the two of us becoming three of us. You're okay about that now, aren't you, Lucy?'

'Yes. Now that you're here with me.'

'I'll always be with you.'

She believed it. She could feel it in her mind, in her heart, in her soul...James, her mate in all things. Lifting back her head, seeing the love in his eyes, the joy of it was so intense, the desire for him so overwhelming, she went up on tip-toes and his mouth met hers…both of them so hungry for each other, there was no stopping the passionate need that seized them.

Ruth Worthington couldn't stop smiling as she moved around her garden with her secateurs and a basket, choosing and snipping off the geranium cuttings her next door neighbour wanted. She felt happier for her daughter than she had ever felt for herself.

Lucy had fallen in love with the right kind of man.

There was no risk to *this* marriage.

No risk at all.

She wondered what kind of wedding Lucy would want. She remembered her own shame, having to select a wedding dress that would cover up her pregnancy. It was different these days. Young women were now proud of showing off their pregnancy, married or unmarried. Lucy could wear any kind of dress she liked. Maybe she would ask Sally Rogan to find something lovely and romantic through her boutique contacts. That would be nice.

A baby…Ruth's smile grew broader…a grandchild. It had been a worry that Lucy would never find someone, never have children. Twenty-eight…good thing she *was* pregnant, starting a family straight away. It just wasn't sensible leaving it too late, especially if Lucy and James ended up deciding to have a bigger family...two or three children. That would be *so* nice.

But...first things first. Whatever Lucy chose for the wedding, it was going to be absolutely perfect with the bride and groom loving each other so much. Which was the most important thing of all. It was what she'd dearly wished for her daughter—what she'd never found herself.

True love.

And that was far, far more than *nice*.

It was wonderful.

VIVA LA VIDA DE AMOR!

They speak the language of passion.

In Harlequin Presents®, you'll find a special
kind of lover—full of Latin charm. Whether
he's relaxing in denims or dressed for dinner,
giving you diamonds or simply sweet dreams,
he's got spirit, style and sex appeal!

Latin Lovers is the new miniseries
from Harlequin Presents® for anyone
who enjoys hot romance!

Meet gorgeous Antonio Scarlatti in
THE BLACKMAILED BRIDEGROOM
by Miranda Lee, Harlequin Presents® #2151
available January 2001

And don't miss sexy Niccolo Dominici in
THE ITALIAN GROOM
by Jane Porter, Harlequin Presents® #2168
available March 2001!

Available wherever Harlequin books are sold.

Lindsay Armstrong...
Helen Bianchin...
Emma Darcy...
Miranda Lee...

Some of our bestselling writers are Australians!

Look our for their novels about the Wonder from Down Under—where spirited women win the hearts of Australia's most eligible men.

THE AUSTRALIANS

Coming soon:

THE MARRIAGE RISK
by Emma Darcy
On sale February 2001, Harlequin Presents® #2157

And look out for:

MARRIAGE AT A PRICE
by Miranda Lee
On sale June 2001, Harlequin Presents® #2181

Available wherever Harlequin books are sold.

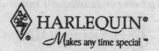

HARLEQUIN®
Makes any time special ™

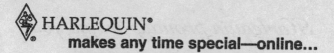